The Music Teacher

This Large Print Book carries the
Seal of Approval of N.A.V.H.

THE MUSIC TEACHER

BARBARA HALL

WHEELER PUBLISHING
A part of Gale, Cengage Learning

GALE
CENGAGE Learning™

Detroit • New York • San Francisco • New Haven, Conn • Waterville, Maine • London

GALE
CENGAGE Learning

LIBRARY OF CONGRESS CATALOGING-IN-PUBLICATION DATA

Hall, Barbara, 1960–
    The music teacher / by Barbara Hall.
      p. cm. — (Wheeler Publishing large print hardcover)
    ISBN-13: 978-1-59722-967-8 (alk. paper)
    ISBN-10: 1-59722-967-9 (alk. paper)
    1. Women violinists—Fiction. 2. Failure (Psychology)—Fiction. 3. Women music teachers—Fiction. 4. Teacher-student relationships—Fiction. 5. Psychological fiction. 6. Large type books. I. Title.
PS3558.A3585M87 2009b
813'.54—dc22   2009000834

Published in 2009 by arrangement with Algonquin Books of Chapel Hill, a division of Workman Publishing Co., Inc.

To my mother, who bought my
first guitar,
and to Bruce, who taught me
what is was for.

"Inspiration is divine.
For everything else there are teachers."

1

I am the mean music teacher. I am that cranky woman you remember from your youth, the one whose face you dreaded seeing, whose breath you dreaded smelling as I leaned over you, tugging at your fingers. You made jokes about me, drew caricatures of me in your notebooks, made puns out of my name, swore never to be me.

Well, listen. I swore never to be me, too.

My name is Pearl Swain. It is my real name. I didn't make it up to give you something to laugh about. My mother chose it for noble reasons. I was named after her mother, a woman she alternately revered and despised. My mother's stories changed with her moods. I tried to stay away from both.

I started playing the violin when I was ten. Two years too late, I was eventually told, to become a great violinist. So I became a very good violinist, which is about like being a very good mathematician. It means you cannot actually make your living at your chosen profession. It means you have to teach others how to surpass you.

Here is why your music teacher was so mean: She didn't want to teach. She wanted to be a musician. She wanted to be first chair in some respectable philharmonic, or onstage with some famous rock band or jazz quartet. She wanted to compose her own pieces and have them published and admired. She wanted an audience for her music, not a succession of surly children being forced to memorize folk tunes and watered-down pop and gospel songs so that their parents could sit through endless recitals and brag about these accomplishments as if they were their own.

Like your music teacher, I am not as old as I appear. I am only forty, and I have aspirations still, circling the drain, but there, nagging and growing louder as they fade. I also have a sex life, or did. Something no one likes to imagine. I have been married and divorced and have been rejected countless other times, and I have even done my share of rejecting. I have bought silly lingerie and cooked impossibly difficult meals and lit candles in the bedroom and used chocolate syrup on things other than ice cream.

But don't think about that. Just know that it's true.

I work in a precious little music shop on the West Side of Los Angeles called Mc-Coy's, named after a Scottish guitar maker, who opened up the place to sell his own handmade guitars and violins, only to be put out of business by the larger chains. He sold the store, and the new management turned the place into a kind of haven for displaced would-be members of Fairport Convention, people who play quaint instruments that no one wants to hear. We sell acoustic guitars, mandolins, violins, cellos, accordions, bongos, recorders, harmonicas, and honest-to-God lutes. The manager, Franklin, tries to pretend that we provide a much-needed service to the area, and he affects an air of disdain for anyone who can't see that, anyone who aspires to play something beyond glorified campfire music.

There is a repair shop, run by Declan Mc-Coy, grandson of the original owner. He rides his bike to work and has a beard down to his diaphragm. There is a back room, where we host small concerts, and there are rooms upstairs where we teach lessons. If you teach, you have to put some hours in working in the shop, selling guitar ⸲ and tuners and sheet music and s'

So in between lessons, I hang out in the store and argue with the other clerks and teachers. I argue the most with Franklin, a decent guitar player who dreams of being a session musician (which is not unlike dreaming of being a ghost writer), and who believes that there are only two guitarists on earth who can even rival him — Alvin Lee and Richard Thompson. Jimmy Page, he says, was only complex, and anybody can be complex if it's the only thing that matters to him. Jimi Hendrix, he says (though he refers to him only as Hendrix), simply reinvented the instrument to suit his purposes. Don't even talk to him about Keith Richards. (I don't know why. I don't care enough.) Eric Clapton is a sellout, Chuck Berry treated his guitar like a car engine (that's a criticism, he swears), and Segovia turned his guitar into a piano, so why the hell didn't he just play the piano?

This is what I listen to all day long. Him arguing with Ernest and Patrick and Clive. They all have rules like this. His are just the stupidest and most cryptic. Ernest hyperventilates over Stevie Ray Vaughan and can't discuss Lynyrd Skynyrd without crying. Patrick says he'd marry Paul Simon if he weren't straight. (I suppose he means if he, Patrick, weren't straight — another lively topic of debate.) Clive, at twenty-eight, is the youngest member of the group, since Franklin won't hire anyone under twenty-five. Clive is a bass player who says that there is no such thing as a great band without a great rhythm section. He says that out loud, whenever Franklin walks by, and if Franklin is in a pleasant mood, he actually pauses to say, "Well, show me the all-rhythm-section band." "The Police," Clive quips, and Franklin holds a hand to his heart, as if he's been shot.

It's all very sad. They are like chess players, arguing over the most valuable piece on the board rather than the beauty of strategy. They are missing the big picture. Musicians often do that. Sometimes I do it, too. We all defend our instruments as if they were extensions of our personalities, which maybe they are, but should we admit it in public? I don't.

Of all the people employed at McCoy's, I make Franklin the craziest. He does not understand me. Mainly because I am a woman. Franklin's musical politics are not unlike those of the Taliban. He probably thinks we should be arrested for playing instruments in public. We're allowed to si⸱ because singers are the lowest of th⸱ We're occasionally relegated to

13

ghetto because the piano, as Franklin puts it, is the dime-store novel of popular music. But when we try to make pleasant sounds come from anything else, we're playing with fire, encroaching on sacred territory.

"Why do you want to play that whiny little thing?" Franklin sometimes asks when he wanders past as I'm warming up before a lesson.

"I didn't choose it," I tell him. "It chose me."

"Only a woman could say that," he replies.

"I am a woman. Where's your argument?"

This actually makes the blood drain from his face, and then he says something like, "Your time card is a mess. Make sure you check your hours," and moves on.

I am in love with Franklin, probably. My fantasy is that he falls in love with me, and I tell him that he should get a real job (he has an MBA from Stanford), and we move to Northern California, play our instruments for fun, and raise five children. This, of course, will never happen. And Franklin has just enough disdain for me that it's safe to fantasize about him. He is not handsome. His hair is deserting him and he's put on ten pounds since I started working here three years ago, right after my divorce. I focused my attention on him as the perfect

14

solution to my problems, since he was so different from my ex-husband, Mark Hooper, a charismatic history professor at UCLA, who eventually gave in to the demands of some lost and weepy coed and tried to blame me for his wanderings. He said it was my desire to be a musician and my refusal to match his salary that created so much stress that he had to look elsewhere for relief. I think he never recovered from the fact that I didn't take his last name. Why would I? As bad as Pearl Swain is, Pearl Hooper is even worse. It sounds like a mail-order gadget. Tired of paying department store prices for jewelry? Try the amazing Pearl Hooper! I did that routine for him and he laughed, but ultimately he saw my refusal to take his name as an act of defiance, as if I were holding back.

Toward the end, he had a million examples like that, little ways that I had hedged my bets, shut him out. He claimed that music was my first love and there was no room for him in my heart. I think that was just a high-minded excuse for sleeping with someone else. Someone much younger, who hung on his every word, loved his big ideas, appreciated the gray in his hair, thought the ev weight looked sexy, thought the wo not appreciate his genius. Someor.

the fictional version of him. Someone who didn't love him enough not to lie.

The truth is that Mark and Franklin are not so different at all. They are both teachers, held back by their own elitist pretensions. Mark hated teaching and believed he should be publishing popular history books. I believed he should be doing that, too. I simply thought it might be good to write those books before he grew embittered over their lack of recognition.

I took the job at McCoy's three months after Mark left me and moved in with Stephanie, the weepy coed, hoping to prove that I could make a living as a musician. It was intended to be the stepping-stone into my actual career as a full-time violinist, but three years later, I am still teaching and pretending it is the same as being a professional musician. Mark didn't get the comeuppance I had hoped for, but every now and then, when I have to call him to discuss money (he's still paying for my car), he says enigmatic and leading things like, "Pearl, you don't know how lucky you are, doing the thing you love."

I say, "Aren't you doing the thing you love?"

"Of course not. You know what I want to 'o."

"You want to write books."

"Yes," he says, sighing.

"So write them."

He says, "Stephanie wants to have children, but we can't afford it."

"What does Stephanie do, again?" I knew, but I never tired of hearing it.

"She's a telemarketer. But she wants to teach."

God help him, he left me for a woman who hasn't even got the courage to teach.

Franklin never gives me a sideways glance, never even acknowledges that I am a woman, except to point out that women make inferior musicians. It's not because I'm ugly. It might be because I have stopped trying to be pretty.

Beauty is work, and expensive work at that. None of the models or actresses in magazines were born with any of that. They might have been born pretty, but nobody is born pretty enough. They've starved themselves, chopped up their faces, sucked the fat out of their butts and put it in their cheeks, and shot botulism into their lips, and after all that, they've still been airbrushed within an inch of their lives. Catch them in a candid moment, and you'll fi someone who's achy, cranky, hungry. exhausted, and full of contempt fc

17

In Los Angeles, these women are everywhere. You can see how miserable they all are. If you don't believe it, try cutting one of their SUVs off in traffic. They don't want to let you in. Pretty people never let you in.

I abandoned all efforts to be pretty after my marriage failed. I used to color my hair; now I just accept what God gave me, something like dull mahogany with no visible gray in a blunt shoulder-length cut. Franklin calls it lesbian hair. Most days I swoop it up in a ponytail or tuck it under a hat. I don't conceal the lines on my forehead (I've earned them) and I don't cover up broken blood vessels on my nose (my ancestors brought them over from Scotland). Sometimes I wear lipstick, but when I do, Franklin calls attention to it. He announces to everyone in the store, "Pearl has feminine aspirations today!"

The only man in the store who seems to appreciate me as I am is young Clive, who occasionally whispers to me, "You know, Joni Mitchell never wore makeup." I say to him, "If I could sing like her, I would tell you all to fuck off."

Clive grins. He likes it when I swear. I don't know why young men find foul-mouthed women so appealing, but they do.

Then Clive says, still speaking of Joni

Mitchell, "She could play the guitar, too. Great rhythm guitar. She was her own rhythm section."

"Don't tell anyone," I caution. "They might confiscate her guitar."

Clive thinks I am supercool because I use words like "confiscate" and I'm not afraid to say "fuck." He really likes the incongruity of my doing all that and playing the violin, which is considered an uptight person's instrument. He likes that I'm not afraid of Franklin and I actually enjoy bands with a rhythm section. I once said to him, "Music is all about timing. If you don't understand that, you don't understand the sport."

Which I believe, but it wasn't really fair to rope him in that way. Ever since then, I think he has made a solemn vow to take a bullet for me.

Clive teaches bass lessons next door to me, and sometimes I hear him yelling at his students. Sometimes I even have to tap on the door and ask him to keep it down. I do this gently, with a forefinger to my lip.

Once, as we were closing up shop, he said to me, "Why don't you ever yell at your students?"

"There's no point," I said.

"But they're so lazy."

"No, they're just frustrated. They're either doing this for their parents, which makes them miserable, or they are doing it for themselves, which makes them even more miserable."

Clive considered that for a moment, rubbing his fingers over his nascent goatee.

"You say smart things," he told me.

"No, I just say stuff out loud. It's why I can't stay married or keep a boyfriend."

"Hey," Clive said, with a degree of adolescent swagger, "if I were a few years older, you wouldn't have a problem."

He thought that was a compliment.

I wasn't always a patient teacher. This is the thing I did not say to Clive because he is too young to understand it. I was too young to understand it before it happened to me. I used to berate my students and raise my voice, and sometimes I would sigh and put my instrument away and say, "I don't see the point of this anymore."

But that was all before Hallie.

If you choose teaching as a profession, or even if you just fall into it as I did, the job is intolerable until you figure out the secret. The secret is this: your student is there to teach you, too. Before Hallie, there were things I believed that were just wrong. Notions of teaching left over from excessive viewing of *The Miracle Worker.* I thought I would reshape their lives. I thought I could teach them all to hear things they had never heard before.

But who can say what occurs between the vibrations of a chord, between the note's leaving the string and the wood and finding a home elsewhere? The child is thinking of other things. The child does not hear these sounds the same way.

I never knew that before. I didn't even bother to think about it.

It was Halloween, a Wednesday, when I first met Hallie. I still mark it on my calendar, and it bothers me that I do that. I wonder what I'm preserving. I wonder if I am making her or myself a martyr.

I had just dismissed my best student, a budding prodigy named Rosamund. She was ten years old and had been playing since she was six, and her parents were certain she was destined for greatness. She was, but only if she wanted it. Rosamund (and you can tell a great deal about parents from the name they choose for their only child) didn't want it. Rosamund wanted to play soccer and climb trees and do math equations. The only reason she unders' anything about the violin was that she

21

math whiz. Musical notation is all math, and that is why many great artists learn to play by ear. Whenever I am called upon to explain that phenomenon, I use this quote: "Some say metaphysics is for people who can't do the math. Others say that metaphysics is for people who don't need to do the math."

That is how I phrase it when I'm sober. When I've got a couple of drinks under my belt, I say, "Music is the closest you will ever get to God. Some people need to have God explained to them through scripture and ritual. Others just go right to the source."

That's why I cut down on drinking.

I had had a difficult session with Rosamund that day because I saw her enthusiasm waning, and instead of letting the whole thing play its course, and because I was convinced I needed her business, I had actually raised my voice to her a little. I said, "Rosamund, you are toiling under the illusion that music is easy. It simply isn't. You have to put in the work. If you don't practice, we are both wasting our time."

"I do practice," she whined to me.

I said, "You practice reading the notes. But you don't practice your bowing. You are doing it mechanically."

I was stifled in my explanation of bowing when it came to children. My usual discourse on how it is done was to say, "It's like sex. It's all feel. If you do it by the numbers, you are going to get caught."

With children, I usually said, "It's like sewing. It's like petting a cat."

But it wasn't. It was like sex.

Which was why they couldn't get it.

Let me just say that in violin playing, bowing is everything. Everything. It is movement, it is feel, it is the voice, it is the stroke, the speed, the timing, the question, the answer, the devil, and the savior. It cannot be overstated. The bow holds the mystery.

None of this matters to a child.

Because Rosamund understood math, she couldn't understand bowing. She could not make the spiritual connection. So I reduced it to the mundane for her. I said, "You have to do those wrist exercises I gave you. You have to keep your wrist supple. Do you know what I mean by 'supple'?"

Pouting, she said, "Yes, but I don't care."

"You need to care."

"So sue me," she said. Language she no doubt learned from her father, who was a litigator and, of course, a frustrated musician.

I wanted to scream at her. I wanted to say,

Do you know what people would give for your talent, not to mention your head start in life? You have a great violin and money for lessons. I started with a shitty violin and a kindhearted housewife for a teacher. If I had had real lessons, so many things might have been different.

But I didn't say any of that. I just said, "See you next week."

I listened to her tromp downstairs, and then I waited for my new student, who had signed up only a week ago. I wasn't sure she'd show. New students mostly didn't show. Ten minutes past her appointment time, I was packing up my things. Then I heard the footsteps on the stairs.

She came into my room upstairs, carrying a battered violin case. She was a young-looking fourteen, with chopped-off black hair and pale skin and a pierced eyebrow. She wore jeans and a faded black T-shirt and Doc Martens. An older woman was with her, and I assumed this to be her mother. The mother was not at all West Side glamorous. She was downtown frumpy in a floral rayon shirt and black sweatpants. The older woman said to me, "This is Hallie Bolaris. She wants to take violin lessons."

"Well, she's come to the right place."

"We can't really afford it, but we're get-

24

ting a grant from the state. It seems she has some kind of talent," the woman said, as if Hallie had an incurable disease.

"Well, I'm sure we can work with that, Mrs. Bolaris," I said.

The woman bristled. "My name is not Bolaris," she said with some degree of urgency. "She is my dead sister's daughter. My sister married a Greek. My name is Mrs. Edwards. Dorothy Edwards."

"Nice to meet you, Mrs. Edwards."

"Hallie is an orphan. We had to take her in when my sister died a few months ago. My sister was living in Sierra Madre."

Sierra Madre is a small town near Pasadena, known for nothing more than being a small town near Pasadena. But the way Dorothy said it, one might have assumed it was a hotbed of illicit activity.

Hallie had no reaction, as if she'd heard this story one too many times.

"Oh. Well, that is a noble thing to do. Adopting your niece."

"I'm not adopted," Hallie said flatly.

"It seems pointless to adopt her," Dorothy explained. "A nightmare of paperwork and legal fees. Plus, she doesn't want to change her name."

"I don't want to be adopted," Hallie said.

"She doesn't want it. That's fine. My

husband and I have children. Two boys. They don't play instruments. They play sports."

"Yes, well, sports are good."

"So how long is this lesson going to be?"

"Our sessions are half an hour, unless you want more . . ."

"That sounds fine." Turning to her niece, she said, "I'll be downstairs, waiting."

She said the word "waiting" as if it were more like giving blood.

When Mrs. Edwards was gone, I turned to Hallie. She was still clutching her battered case.

"Is there an instrument in there?"

Hallie said, "Yeah, it's my father's."

"Your father . . . who is no longer with us?"

"He died when I was seven."

"But he taught you how to play?"

"No, he just gave it to me and told me I could do whatever I wanted to with it."

"So you don't know how to play."

She shrugged. "I play all right."

"Well, take it out and let's see."

Hallie removed an equally battered violin from her case. It was made of cheap wood and had seen happier days, but I could tell it had been played. And if a wood instrument has been played, that's half the battle.

I will tell you why, though you might not care. A musician is used to that — caring to an outrageous degree about something everyone else ignores. For the average guy, music is simply there. Available every time he hits a button. But before it hits these frequencies, music travels on another frequency altogether — that is, the friction created by strings against wood, air against brass, wood against wood, and so on. Waves. Vibrations. Vibrations are good for any organic thing. Wood comes to life when it is vibrated, dies when it isn't. I love this about musical instruments. They have lives. They have moods. They are at risk. They want to be played.

"Do you know how to hold it?" I asked her.

She raised her pierced eyebrow at me, then tucked the instrument directly under her chin, as bluegrass fiddlers do.

I said, "Play me what you know."

She sighed and played a bored version of "Amazing Grace." She hit the notes perfectly, indicating a good ear, and she moved the bow with a great deal of promise.

"Very nice," I said. "How many lessons have you had?"

"None."

"None?"

"Right."

"But who taught you that? Your father?"

"Nope."

"Then who?"

"Nobody."

"What do you mean?"

"I just figured it out."

Now my heart started to race. If my guess was right, I had encountered one of those rare students who has a genuine ear for music. She didn't need to do the math. This is different from a student who has a knack, a proclivity, or even a talent. A student with a natural ear is what you need to create a star. We all secretly want to create a star. We all want Jacqueline du Pré to walk into our office. We want to bend her and shape her and stretch her and maybe, down the road, get a little credit.

I never liked to admit that about myself as a teacher. But at least I wasn't one of those teachers who tries to kill talent. Those exist in large numbers, and not unlike Scientologists or Freemasons, it would frighten you to know how many there are.

Me, I just wanted to run along next to the promise and the glory, get sucked into its force, feel the wind of someone else's accomplishment on my face. These are the dark, ugly secrets of teaching I am telling you. Pay attention.

"Can you read music?" I asked.

Again she shrugged. "Yeah, but it slows me down."

My heart raced faster.

I said, "Who are your heroes?"

"My what?" she asked impatiently.

"The people you attempt to emulate on your instrument."

She shrugged. "I don't have any heroes."

"None at all?"

"No."

"Joshua Bell? Itzhak Perlman?"

"Who?"

I smiled. "Tell me one person whose violin playing has inspired you."

She thought about it for a moment, and I watched her. Her face seemed malleable, as if it were made of clay. Young people often seem that way to me. Unfinished, unde-fined, hard to recognize in a crowd. Facial features could take a wrong turn any minute, or a right one, rendering the pretty face ugly or the ugly face pretty, without warning, without logic.

"I like Bruce Springsteen."

I nodded. Then I said, "Well, Bruce doesn't really play the violin."

"Yeah, but like on that song, 'Jungleland.' He has a violinist on that number. I like how she sounds."

"Yes. I do, too."

"And then there's the Charlie Daniels Band. That song, 'The Devil Went Down to Memphis.' "

I said, "Yes, I know that song. But I think it's Georgia."

"What's Georgia?"

"Georgia is the place the devil went down to."

She tucked the instrument under her arm and said, "To tell you the truth, I hate playing this thing. I wish I could put it in a trash can. You know? Like a dead baby. I never want to see it again."

I nodded. "Yes, I know how that feels, too."

She twirled her bow between her fingers, like a baton, wary of the possibility that I might understand her.

And I didn't understand her all that well, because I wanted to say, No, don't do that. You're not supposed to touch the hairs on a violin bow. You're supposed to treat the bow like a sacred artifact. Partly because it's expensive to have the bow restrung (or, more accurately, rehaired). But mainly because the bow holds all the mysteries. The bow is the thing. It's the Eucharist. It can work miracles.

I stopped myself from correcting her, but she saw the stress on my face.

"Why should I play this thing?" she asked me.

"I don't know. What else are you going to do? Get stoned? Get laid?"

"Yeah," she said. "I might rather do both of those things."

Her defiant stance told me that she had never come close to doing either of those things. But this is an area you are not allowed to comment on while teaching an instrument.

"I might rather, too," I said. "But it all ends up in the same place. You wake up in the morning knowing how to do something that a billion other people know how to do. But if you wake up knowing a new song on the violin, then you're different."

"I'm different enough," she informed me.

"You have a gift," I said, trying not to oversell it. Teachers learn that nothing alienates certain teenagers like encouragement and enthusiasm.

She stared at me a long time, then tucked the instrument under her chin again. She said, "Every half hour I spend here is a half hour I don't have to spend at home. So let's go."

2

Franklin walks me to my car. It is a November evening and the sun is going down at a ridiculous hour. Franklin has decided I am not safe. I don't know if he thinks I'm going to be attacked and raped or stopped on the street and asked to prove myself as a musician. He is carrying his Taylor guitar in a gig bag, slung over his shoulder. I have my violin in a hard case, carrying it by the handle. If a poet were to drive by on Pico Boulevard, he would dream up this title: "Two Musicians, Walking Home, Disappointed."

Franklin says, "I think I am going to reconfigure the sales people."

I say, "Oh? You're going to fire someone?"

Franklin says, "Ernest is good on the floor, and so is Patrick, but Clive is a problem."

"Why is he a problem?"

"He talks people out of sales."

"Everybody at McCoy's does that."

Franklin frowns. He knows what I think of his sales technique. He thinks people should have to audition to shop there. They aren't good enough to take these instruments home, and they would mistreat them.

"Okay," he says, "then he aggressively does it. He succeeds more than the rest of us, how's that?"

"So he's getting fired for being better than us?"

"Do you want to hear this or not?"

"I'm listening."

"He chases them away by lecturing them on the rhythm section. You know him and the rhythm section."

"It's what he believes in. Let him have it. He's patient behind the cash register and he probably knows more about music than either one of us."

"He's a kid," Franklin says.

It's true. He is a kid. He is literally wide eyed and handsome in a raw and disorienting way. Like most young men, he is more head than body. He wears torn T-shirts and torn jeans and he pretends to forget to comb his hair. He comes across all loose and jagged, but he is a rule follower, as if he's scared of being kicked out of school. His time card is always neatly punched and his lessons are all accounted for. He never borrows anything from the store (though the rest of us do), and he tells us weeks ahead when he wants to take a day off. He's the model employee.

"He works hard. He's a good teacher," I say.

Franklin sighs and asks, "Why do you defend him?"

We are at my car now, a block away from the store on noisy Pico Boulevard, where people drive angrily and fast and will hit you for a doughnut. I unlock the door and put my violin in the back. We talk in raised voices over the din of traffic. "Because I like him," I say.

Franklin smirks. "You only like him because he likes you."

"I can't imagine a better reason."

Franklin's face goes red again, and he says, "You fall for his crap."

"I listen to what he says. Some of it I agree with, some of it I don't. That's all. But it's worth asking yourself why you dislike him so much."

"I just think he's bad at his job."

"He isn't. You think he's a bad musician."

"Isn't it the same thing?"

I smile, leaning against my worn-out Honda. "No, Franklin, it's not. We aren't professional musicians. We work in a music store. And Clive has more students than all of us."

He runs that through his head, doing the figures. He says, "He has fourteen. Same as you."

"I have thirteen."

"Since when?"

"I don't teach Hallie Bolaris anymore."

He seems surprised by this information. He knew Hallie, as all the people in McCoy's did, because she came in so often (never missed a lesson, and sometimes took extras), and because her unofficially adopted mother, Mrs. Edwards, used to amuse the people in the store while she waited for Hallie to finish. Mrs. Edwards hated music and wasted no time in telling everyone that. Sometimes she would hover over Declan as he repaired instruments. She'd say to him, "Let me ask you something. Why do you have such a long beard?"

Declan, easily the most even tempered and well adjusted of the McCoy's employees, said, "Because I don't like to shave."

Mrs. Edwards said, "I don't like to clean the toilet, but it has to be done."

Declan said, "I like to clean the toilet. I do it with my beard."

That pretty much finished their relationship. She moved on to Ernest, who often played guitar on the floor when business was slow. She'd watch him, unable to stop herself from being drawn in by his playing, which was quite impressive.

She'd say to him, "You look like a smart young man. Why are you wasting your time in a music store?"

Ernest said, "I tried wasting it in other places, but I usually got arrested."

This was true of Ernest. He was a real musician, which meant that he had encountered (and overcome) serious substance-abuse problems. Most real musicians don't overcome them, or didn't in my day. No one of my generation ever expected to see Keith Richards or Eric Clapton welcome in the new millennium. We are all still a bit thrown by that, which is why we sometimes refer to them as sellouts.

Pretty soon, Hallie and Dorothy had become the stuff of legend at McCoy's. People looked forward to Wednesdays, when Hallie came, because they were certain to be entertained. It was Hallie who indirectly instituted the Wednesday night discussion group, wherein all the employees of McCoy's would hang around telling funny stories about our exploits, and then we'd move on to talk of music, and eventually we would play instruments and wouldn't end up leaving the shop until around midnight.

We no longer had the Wednesday night discussion group because it went away when Hallie did. I'm the only one at McCoy's who makes that connection. Everyone else thinks we all just got busy, even though nobody's any busier.

"What happened to Hallie?" he asks.

"I don't know."

"She just disappeared?"

"Something like that."

"Did she say why?"

Did she say why? She did and she didn't.

Did I know why?

I did and I didn't.

"No, she never told me. Directly. Her mother said something. Her foster mother. It was complicated."

Franklin's face registers a modicum of concern for me. In the old days, I would have mistaken it for love. But the reason I am alone now is that I've learned to tell the difference.

"You said she was your best student."

"She was more than that. She had the potential to be great. The way she understood the instrument."

"Better than you?"

"Yes, much better than me. Maybe that's why she stopped coming. Because I had nothing left to teach her."

Franklin doesn't want to hear this. He shakes his head and shifts his guitar up on his shoulder. He clings to that guitar as if it were a security blanket. It is a security blanket. That is what all our instruments are to us. The difference between me and Franklin is that I know it.

"She was just a kid," he says. "I'm sure she just got bored."

Franklin appears to be stuck in this place where youth is the enemy. Maybe it's resentment; maybe it's envy. Maybe he thinks that young people have the gift of opportunity awaiting them, while the truth is that like anyone else, they have to wade through the mud of confusion before they can confront the landscape of possibility.

But I let him think it was her youth that led her down the sinkhole, because the truth is too hard. There are two possible scenarios. In one, I am crazy. In the other, I am cruel. Time does not smooth out the edges of those choices.

I stare at the cars moving past in erratic colors like pills. The colors don't mean anything. It's just how you tell one from the other.

I say, "What do you think it means when the scriptures say unless you're like a child you can't enter the kingdom of heaven? Jesus couldn't have been talking about innocence or happiness or painlessness."

Franklin looks at me as if I'm not well.

"I don't think about the scriptures, Pearl. Why do you?"

"I don't know. Because I'm from the South. I was raised with it."

"I was raised with a lot of crazy ideas I've left behind," he says.

"It doesn't seem like a crazy idea. It seems like a mysterious one."

"You're not from the South. You're from Virginia."

"Last capital of the Confederacy. Danville, Virginia. My hometown. That's not the South? I will drop them a note."

Franklin is almost done with me now. He doesn't like to talk about the South. He doesn't want too much truth at once. Who does? The fact is, I am from a real place, with a real musical heritage. He is from a land that someone dreamed, and the dream is not complete. California is still entirely open to interpretation. The South has been defined. It has gone to war. California has gone to skirmish. It is still looking for a war. In the interim, its contradictions are played out on the battlegrounds of music and art and status. Los Angeles is swollen with hope and infected with aspiration. But there are good places to eat and an ocean.

He starts away, then turns back. He says, "Hey, Pearl, it's eleven hours before the world ends. What kind of music do you play on the violin?"

"Bluegrass," I tell him.

This surprises him. Franklin fancies himself a bluegrass guitar player. He thinks I fancy myself a classical musician. But I am curiously devoid of knowledge in that area. I present the music to my students — the cold, complicated sheets of notation required to emulate the greats. But I cleave to the mountain music, the made-up stuff, the accident of passion converging on intellectual restriction. The marriage of ignorance and ideals. This is where music is really found.

Franklin doesn't accept that being born in the wrong place is keeping him from making truly beautiful sounds come out of his guitar. That's why he wants to be a session musician. That's what you do when you give up.

"You? Bluegrass?" he asks, his face an open question mark.

"Sure."

"Why?"

"Because eleven hours before the world ends, I'd want to be close to God."

He has nothing to say to that. He turns on his heel and walks away. I watch him go, his guitar bumping against his hip, nagging him, as a good woman might do.

There is nothing in my place when I get home. I used to have a cat, but it scared me too much to be a single music teacher with a cat. The cat's name was Roy. Roy used to mock me. I can't explain how. He just did. I had named him after Roy Orbison, which was probably my first mistake. I love Roy Orbison, but he was a tragic figure. His wife died in a motorcycle accident, and two of his children died in a house fire. He never got over their loss. It was why he made such beautiful music. It was why he died in his fifties, just as his career was taking off again. His heart was worn out; he couldn't take it anymore. When that happens, we call it a heart attack. But the heart never attacks. It simply breaks.

One day, back when I was teaching Hallie and obsessed with her progress, I went to work without closing the patio door in my apartment. Roy ran away. Can you blame him? I couldn't. But I did attempt to look for him, put up flyers, the whole thing. My landlord, a disheveled old hippie alcoholic named Steve, approached me in the lobby one day and said, "Pearl, I know you want to find your cat, but the truth is, you aren't supposed to have pets in this building. It's, like, policy."

"You don't have to worry, Steve. Roy isn't coming back. I just had to make an effort to find him."

"If I'd known you had a pet, I wouldn't have leased the apartment."

I said, "If I'd known you were an alcoholic, I wouldn't have signed the lease."

Steve left me alone after that. Sometimes you have to use the truth in that way. God forgives it.

Shortly after that, I moved. I like to think it was because I needed a change. I prefer not to think that I was running from the ghost of Roy. But my new home is a dead and lonely place where I still think of Roy. Just as my job feels like a dead and lonely place where I still think of Hallie. I do my level best not to obsess about her. I usually have several glasses of wine when I come home, and eventually I get drunk enough and bored enough with what's on television to put a frozen dinner in the microwave. I usually overcook it, then I eat it, and then I scrape up the burned bits with a fork and eat that, too.

This takes up a lot of energy, so I eventually get into the bathtub and I go to bed. When I fall asleep, things get weird. Because I dream. It's the only time I allow myself to dream, and I wouldn't even allow it then if I could help it. But as a student of mine once said, "My brain has a mind of its own." I dream of my past, in Danville, Virginia, and I dream of my future, in Los Angeles, California, and the two worlds don't like each other much. I toss and turn and grind my teeth. I broke a molar once. Sometimes I even sleepwalk. Or sleep-run. I woke up, just a few weeks ago, running around my living room. When I came to, I felt foolish. I was wearing sweatpants and a tank top. I was saying out loud, "There is no such thing as fire. There is no such thing as fire."

It's funny, at least to me, that I woke up saying, "There is no such thing as fire."

My father, a carpenter by trade, knew all about fire. He knew about it because he knew about wood. He knew which kind would burn under what conditions. He even knew that if you vacuumed sawdust the vacuum cleaner would catch fire, something to do with the sparks in the motor creating combustion in the wood. He knew what

43

would start a fire and what would stop it. He knew how fire behaved, how it moved, what made it advance and turn back. And once a fire got big enough, he cautioned me, "Don't try to fight it. It's going to win."

It created confusion, his stories about wood and fire. You'd think a friend of the wood would hate the fire, but he didn't. He respected it. He saw beauty in it. Not in the aesthetic, I imagine, because he never cared for colors that I could tell. But in its powers of destruction, which I suppose he saw as a creative act.

Maybe people in his generation had been told the stories of Sherman's March to the Sea and had never recovered. Maybe he knew a thousand things I couldn't know because of his strange, sad past full of poverty and scandal and things he had done to pull himself out and still couldn't talk about to the day he died.

I wondered what he would think if I told him there was no such thing as fire.

Before he died, when we used to talk about politics in quick, painful bursts, he tried to tell me there were no homeless people in America. And if there were, they had done something to deserve it. Not like his people. They had done nothing to deserve poverty, but this generation was different. His generation had had wars and depressions and all. We had no such legacy.

Hallie was homeless. Not in the traditional sense, of course. She was being taken care of by Aunt Dorothy, but she had not really known what a home felt like. Her parents had died too young. Because they had lived too hard. Her father was a gifted musician, and he checked out when she was seven. Her mother had hung in there for as long as possible, but she was a struggling singer-turned-artist. She sang like an angel, Hallie told me. After her husband died, she stopped singing and started to paint. Because Hallie's mother had gotten so close to God, as singers and artists often do, she had elected to check out. Hallie's mother was a heroin addict. Hallie didn't tell me that. Her adopted mother did.

She told me one Wednesday when Hallie showed up for a lesson. Unpacking her violin, Hallie realized she had left her rosin for the bow in the car. She excused herself and went out to get it.

Dorothy said to me, "The child has seen hard times, you know."

"Yes," I said.

"Her mother was a drug addict."

"That's terrible," I said. I didn't really think it was so terrible. I thought it was

45

simply a choice. But I said that in order to get Dorothy to talk. It worked.

"Heroin," Dorothy whispered to me. Sitting up straight, she said, "And there was no excuse for it. My sister was a brilliant artist."

"A violinist?" I asked.

"No, an artist. Like with paint. She painted beautiful pictures. But art is expensive, you know? She married a horrible man, thinking he would support her, but all he did was drink himself to death."

"He was a musician?"

"He was a scoundrel. Cheated on my sister and bled her dry."

I nodded. I understood. I said, "What happened to her art?"

Dorothy took a breath and said, "She had just painted a series of pictures that were getting a lot of attention. She painted musicians. She went out into the streets of Sierra Madre and she painted people playing their guitars. Then she just started painting guitars. They were beautiful, brightly colored things. Celebrities started to buy them. They did a piece on her for a news show. She was making money and she was starting to get famous . . ."

Dorothy stopped. But I wasn't ready to quit.

"What happened?"

Dorothy shrugged. "What happens with all you people? She started using drugs, and one day they found her. Curled up in a ball in the bathroom. Dead from an overdose."

"Who found her?" I asked.

Dorothy knew what I was asking.

"Hallie found her."

Then we heard Hallie's footsteps on the stairs, and we both sat in silence as Hallie emerged, holding nothing in her hands.

"I left my rosin at home," she said.

"That's all right," I told her. "I can rosin your bow. Let's just get started."

Dorothy looked at me, connecting, and then said in that long-suffering way, "I'll be downstairs."

And so she was. Always waiting.

I pour myself another glass of wine and turn on the news and stare at it for a long time before turning it off again.

It is quiet and I'm listening for instruction.

I hear a voice somewhere. It says, Account for Hallie.

And I say to the voice, Give me an easier task.

The voice says no.

3

When you get a student like Hallie, you have to make a decision.

Will you make her great?

Actually, that comes at the end of several small decisions, the first of which is, Will I teach her at all? Will I invest myself? Will I put in all the work and the hope? Once you have made the decision, nothing can stop you. Because it is no longer about the student. Now it is about the teacher. The teacher makes a choice to live her ambitions through a person other than herself. To invest in your student is in many ways to let go of your own dream.

Parents do this all the time with their children. And it fucks them up. I know, because I teach those kids. And when I made the decision to teach Hallie, I suddenly understood the ambitious parents. It's far too hard to let a dream die completely. Before you do that, you will pass it on to another person, whether she wants it or not.

Hallie wanted it. She would come into the lesson room looking like something that cat dragged in, pale with red-rimmed eyes and matted hair. Her expression was a kaleidoscope of anger, indifference, resignation, and desire. She would argue with me for the first ten minutes of the lesson. About anything and everything. Sometimes she would announce, "I didn't practice. I hate practicing." When I said that was fine, she'd come up with something else. She'd say, "I hate this fucking instrument, and the only reason I'm playing it is to piss off my so-called parents."

I'd say, "Well, that's as good a reason as any to play music. What do you think got Bruce Springsteen started? You think his parents were pleased as punch to have a rock musician in the family?"

Once, she considered this and smiled. "I'll bet they're happy to have a rock star in the family now."

"Well, yeah," I said. "And that's one reason he did it. To show them."

Her face deflated, and she said, "I don't want to show them anything."

"Not now. Maybe later."

And then we got down to studying.

Sometimes she'd tell me about her family.

49

Once, in between songs, she said, "You have no idea what it's like to live in my house."

I smiled and said, "Bet I do."

"Did you like your parents?"

"Sometimes. I like them now because they are dead."

Her face came alive with interest.

"How'd they die?" she asked.

"My mother died of a stroke just a few years ago. My father died ten years ago, from cancer. But he had been dying a long time."

"How?" she asked.

"I don't think he ever really liked being alive."

"Why?"

"Because he'd given up on so many things."

"What things?"

I didn't know how to tell her what things. My father's past was a mystery to me, and his present wasn't much easier to under- stand. But he was angry, and most of that rage flew in circles and swooped like a bat toward anything beautiful. Music in particu- lar. He didn't want anyone to have it, which I figured meant he must have wanted it at some time and was forced away from it. By what? Overly religious parents or some ambitions he didn't even possess? The woman he married? I remembered him talking, too, about being good at art when he was in school. But then he went into the army. And then it all dropped off into the confusion of my own existence.

I didn't say any of this to her because no matter how tempting it might become, you do not use your students as therapists.

I did say something like this: "I think he had a talent of some kind and he misplaced it."

"How do you do that?" she asked.

"So many ways, Hallie. So many."

But she just rolled her eyes at me and started in on her scales. She thought I was talking about practicing.

Patrick is the only person in the store when I come in. Patrick is mostly quiet, doing his bit in the store and recording music (he says) in his spare time. He has an interesting history, we've all decided, though we don't know what it is. He doesn't play in a band. He doesn't come from money. (He's from the Midwest, we think, the son of a farmer.) Maybe he has a second job, but if he does, he doesn't talk about it. Patrick doesn't talk about anything. When he does talk, he speaks in a slow twang, and his long eyelashes flutter. This is why everyone

51

speculates as to his sexual preference. That and the Hawaiian shirts he insists on wearing nearly every day. Franklin and Ernest brag about their exploits with women, and Clive gets his heart broken about once a week by the same woman, who simply will not commit to being with a poor musician. So they feel they are safe. Another thing they don't trust about Patrick is that he won't identify what instrument he plays. We know he plays something because he talks so knowledgeably about music and can sight-read, but he doesn't teach lessons, and no one has ever seen him pick up an instrument.

"It's just theory," Franklin sometimes speculates. "He's just a music-theory nerd. He doesn't play anything. He's one of those weirdos who reads music but can't do anything with it."

"So why do you keep him on?" asks Ernest, who feels that everyone should justify their existence at McCoy's, as if we were all working at NASA. Ernest, as a Texan, somehow equates playing an instrument with fist fighting. Not for the soft or cowardly. He doesn't trust anyone who uses a capo on a guitar — a fact that he once whispered to me when Franklin was across the room, showing off on a Martin signature series of some kind. Franklin loved the capo. He had dissertations about the importance of the capo. Ernest said, "If your hand can't grab the chord, then walk the fuck away from it."

Do you see what I'm saying? Do you see?

Back when we had the Wednesday night discussion group, Patrick always stayed but never discussed anything. He simply hung around to listen. He leaned against the counter and smiled at our impassioned debates, rarely offering an opinion. Sometimes he laughed when things got particularly heated, and this would make Franklin angry.

"You think music is funny? Is that what you think?"

"Well, a little bit," Patrick would say in his deliberate, nasally tone. "But I think most things are funny."

"Maybe if you actually played an instrument, you'd understand how serious it is."

"Maybe so," Patrick would say. He knew the rule. If you want to drive someone crazy, just keep agreeing with him. Franklin would give up on arguing with him, and then the playing would start. When Ernest and Clive and Franklin and I played, Patrick would get a sad, dreamy, faraway look in his eyes, as if he were remembering a better time.

Had he once known how to play an instrument? Had he lost that ability, like someone who had lost the ability to walk or speak?

When he lets me in, Patrick says, "Hey, Pearl. How's it going?"

"Pretty good. How's it going with you?"

"Not bad," he says.

We're like some Protestant family that has learned not to discuss anything substantial.

Patrick is my age, with hair down to his shoulders, which he sometimes pulls back into a ponytail. He has a nice white trash kind of face and scary blue eyes. My own eyes are green, but I feel like I can't trust anyone with light-colored eyes. It's as if we aren't finished.

He reminds me of Townes Van Zandt. I say to him, this particular morning, "You remind me of Townes Van Zandt."

Townes Van Zandt is a martyr for anyone who appreciates music in the country / bluegrass / alternative rock realm. He was a poet who wrote and recorded songs that made you want to open a vein. Born in Fort Worth, Texas, and a lifelong alcoholic, he died suddenly following hip surgery. When he died, his daughter is purported to have said, "Daddy had an argument with his heart." He would have liked that description.

Patrick smirks and says, "Thanks."

"What? You don't like Townes Van Zandt?"

He says, "Well, yeah. I kind of like the dentist, too, because I'm mildly attracted to pain. But you can't take it every day."

"So you listen to him every six months?"

"About like that."

I move to the cash register and start counting the private lesson tickets that have not been incorporated into the financial well. Patrick stands next to me, watching.

Patrick says, "If you're keeping score, you still have the most private lessons."

"It's not a competition. But Clive is ahead of me."

"It's not a competition? Around here? Don't tell anybody."

I lose count, then start again. As I near the end, I turn to him and say, "Why don't you have any students?"

Patrick shrugs and says, "I hate teaching. Why do you have so many students?"

"Because I don't hate teaching."

He laughs. I don't know how to respond to that. So I say, "You could make more money if you taught lessons."

"I don't care much about money."

"Don't you have to worry about rent?"

"No. I don't have to worry about that. I don't have to worry about anything. Neither do you."

"Are you getting all Buddhist on me or something?"

"Oh, no," he says, as if the talk has suddenly turned serious. "I was raised Lutheran. But I'm religiously unaffiliated."

"Why don't you have to worry about rent?" I ask.

Patrick shakes his head, as if he only wants to clear the hair from his face.

I say, "Patrick, everyone wants to know your story."

He smiles. "Everyone wants to find the Holy Grail. But to do that, you have to get on a horse."

"Okay, whatever," I say as I put the lesson tickets away.

Patrick leans against the counter, looks at me, and says, "Pearl, why do you take him on?"

"Who?"

"Franklin. Why do you want to prove anything to him?"

"I don't want to prove anything. I just want to keep my job."

"You have your job. Franklin would never fire you. He's in love with you."

"No, he's not. Don't say that."

It doesn't matter how much I love Franklin. I want to be employed for my talent.

Patrick smiles. His long eyelashes float down, then back up.

He says, "The whole dilemma between men and women is they've tried all the configurations and now they're bored. The genders are out of ideas."

I say, "So what? People run out of ideas. It happens. Your beloved Paul Simon ran out of ideas. So he went to South Africa to get some new ones. That's where *Graceland* came from. A dearth of ideas."

He laughs. "You aren't going to get me on that one. I don't care enough to argue."

"Why not?"

Patrick says, "I was talking about relationships between men and women. You abruptly shifted. You're trying to figure me out. You're looking for clues."

"Clues? I don't think you're that much of a puzzle."

"No, I'm not. I just have a policy. Wait until asked."

"And what, no one ever asks?"

"No one ever does," he says, and goes away whistling.

I can't resist. He is making me do it: "Okay, Patrick. What instrument do you play?"

He turns and smiles. "All of them."

"What do you mean, 'all of them'?"

Still smiling: "None of them."

"Which is it?"

"It's both," he says, and disappears behind the books.

I had no hopes of Hallie's showing for our second lesson. Hallie was not what we call in violin-teaching parlance a sure thing. A sure thing is a student whose parents are so invested in their child's musical future that they force him or her to take lessons. This works until the child enters the early teens. Then the child becomes rebellious, starts acting out. She (I say "she," because it is usually girls who are saddled with this particular burden) stops practicing, starts back-talking the teacher, and generally self-destructs. Not long after that, she examines other outlets for her frustration and turns to cigarettes, drugs, alcohol, bad grades, crime — or sometimes the guitar. At this point the parents become overwhelmed by the situation at hand, and they tell the teacher, in desperate tones, "We simply don't have time for this anymore. We have bigger problems." That's when the music teacher says something like, "Stick with the violin. It's the way out." But the parents have lost faith in music by then. They have turned to counseling, discipline, prescription drugs, or organized religion, all of which roads lead them further into hell.

The less traveled path is that the student's enthusiasm for music actually takes off, and by the time she reaches her late teens, she is obviously destined for an actual career in music. At this point the teacher becomes desperate. Here the teacher is faced with a person who is going to embark on the career that she herself has abandoned. It is too hard to face. So the teacher becomes angry and demanding and generally unhelpful. And the parents decide it's not working out, or the student becomes aware that the teacher is no longer interested in teaching, and it all comes to an end.

Maybe they go off and find better teachers. They must. I never get to know what happens after students leave McCoy's. That is, I've never cared enough to try. Except once.

After Hallie, I stopped trying to inhibit my students. I just encourage them, at all levels, for any reason. I don't make them practice and I don't yell at them and I don't put up a fuss when they talk about quitting. Which is why I now have the most students.

Hallie did show up for the second lesson, ten minutes late. I was already packing up, as I had been doing the first time she showed up. Her adopted mother escorted her into the room and said, "How long is this going to take?"

I said, "Mrs. Edwards, it always takes half an hour. But if you show up ten minutes late, it only takes twenty minutes. Which means you have cheated yourself out of the full lesson."

Mrs. Edwards smirked. "I'm not cheating anybody. None of this was my idea. And anyway, it's the state's money."

I said, "Then you are cheating Hallie."

Hallie looked at me. Which was quite something to behold. Her dark eyes rarely landed on a single location for any amount of time.

Mrs. Edwards, whose face had turned a funny shade of pink, said, "Hallie should understand that everything she gets is icing on the cake. She should show some grati-tude."

I looked at Hallie. "Are you grateful for your music lessons?"

Hallie shrugged, looked away from me again, as if I were the enemy.

"You see?" Mrs. Edwards asked me.

"Please wait downstairs," I told her.

And Mrs. Edwards left.

Hallie was left standing there, holding her violin case. She was staring a hole in the worn-out carpet, which couldn't really use any more holes.

I told her to take out her instrument, and she did. She stood there while I tuned it, then checked the rosin on the bow. Everything was in order.

I said, "This instrument holds its tune very well."

Which was unusual, I didn't add, for an instrument of such poor quality.

Hallie said, "Yeah, I keep it tuned."

"What do you mean?"

She shrugged. "I tune it."

I wasn't sure how to respond. I had not taught her how to tune the instrument for a few reasons. One is that it is extremely difficult to tune a violin. If you don't know what you're doing, you will break a string. A violin string is expensive — nine bucks a pop — so I don't encourage my kids to try this until their parents (or whoever is paying for the lessons) are firmly committed.

The other is that unless you have an electronic tuner, a tuning fork, or another tuned instrument at hand, you simply can't do it. Unless you have a perfect ear. Perfect pitch. Something like 2 percent of the population has that. I have relative pitch, the next best thing, but I don't tell anyone. It makes people crazy. It's like telling someone you can see the future.

And so when Hallie said that, I knew she was 2 percent of the population, and I knew it was a secret she had been keeping, to ensure her own survival.

"Sit down, Hallie," I said.

She sat. She turned her ankles on their sides as she looked at me.

"Close your eyes," I said.

She blinked at me. Her eyebrow ring glinted in the light.

"Why? That's weird."

"Just indulge me," I said.

She closed her eyes.

I played the open-string D.

"What note is that?" I asked.

She hesitated, her eyes still closed. "How do I know?"

"Just guess," I said.

"Play it again," she requested.

I did.

Without opening her eyes, she said, "D."

I tried it again all over the scale, notes out of order. She got them all right. I told her to open her eyes. She might have noticed that the color had drained from my face.

I said, "How did you know that?"

She shrugged. "I read it in a book."

"Read what in a book?"

She said, "What the notes are."

"Yes, but how do you hear them out of relation?"

She grew agitated, started chewing on a hangnail. She wouldn't answer.

So I said, "How do you know it, just by hearing it?"

She sighed, let her hands drop to her lap. "I hear stuff, all right?"

"What stuff?" I asked.

She looked me in the eye, and it was scary. There was something about her gaze that threatened to expose everything. I didn't look away, but I could imagine why most people did.

She said, "There's this department store my mother used to take me to, when I was little. It made me crazy. It made my head hurt. Because I could hear this high buzzing sound. I asked her what it was. She couldn't hear anything. But I just kept bugging her about it till she asked one of the clerks. The clerk said, 'There's a high-frequency security system in here. Nobody can hear it. But it gives some people headaches. Maybe that's what's happening to your daughter.' "

I just stared at her. But because I didn't look away, she kept talking.

She said, "My mother explained about the headaches, but I said, I don't have a headache. It just hurts my ears. I can hear it."

"All right," I said slowly. I had never had an experience like that, but when I was little, I had had a similar problem. I could hear people talking at great distances. I could hear my parents talking in another room, downstairs. I could hear our neighbors talking. Which was quite a feat, if you consider that we didn't live in a cheap apartment building with thin walls. We lived in a house, with several yards separating one house from another.

I tried telling my mother once, and it frightened her so much I never mentioned it again. She told me in no uncertain terms that what I was suggesting was impossible. So I went along with her version of reality and made it impossible.

After that, I started to hear people's thoughts.

But I had never, ever told anyone that.

And I eventually stopped doing it. It was too scary.

All this talk about seeing into people's souls. That's nothing. Try hearing it.

I spent the rest of the lesson just playing notes for Hallie, as she sat in the chair, her eyes closed. I played the notes all up and down the scales. Sharps, flats, naturals. She identified them all. It turned into a game. We started to laugh. We were laughing, in fact, when Mrs. Edwards tapped on the door and stuck her head in.

"I have to get dinner started," she said.

Hallie opened her eyes and looked at me. I smiled at her. She didn't smile back, but it didn't matter. The connection was solid. There was no turning back.

4

There is an open mic at McCoy's the first Sunday of every month, like Communion. Open mics can be a dangerous and horrible thing. You are exposing yourself to the possibility of musical crimes being committed on hallowed ground. All honest musicians despise the concept of the open mic. Untrained people come, and if they are bad, you feel they are defecating on your property. If they are good, you feel they are showing you that you've been defecating on your property. Nothing positive can come from it, though we all pretend it's important to foster the idea of musical community.

McCoy's tolerates the open mic because it is good for business. Open your doors, with the promise of a PA system, and people will come. They will come lugging guitars and saxophones and bongos. They will sing or speak or gyrate or pray their emotions for the entire world, or at least for the small audience, to hear. I hate the open mic, as any real musician does, but I go along with it because Franklin says it is good for the store.

McCoy's open mic is legendary. We have somehow managed to convince people that only the accomplished players should show their faces. The employees kick the evening off by playing their instruments, setting the standard, showing the would-be musicians that they are most likely out of their league. We usually manage to discourage people. Sometimes the odd maniac leaks through.

The maniac on our particular circuit is a man who calls himself Billy Beelzebub. Billy is a slim man in his late twenties who can barely play his untuned Telecaster, and he allows himself to be accompanied by a drunk fiddle player named Louise, who is so bad she is almost endearing. The only reason they don't get booed off the stage is that Billy wears a very expensive cowboy hat and is an accomplished lyricist. He can't play for shit, but his words are funny and he has actually accumulated a small cult following.

On the nights that Billy shows up, he goes on last. He likes to go on last. He thinks he is sending a message this way. We allowed him to do that for years, but in recent months, Franklin has insisted on playing the closing number. He always plays Doc Watson's "Windy and Warm," which leaves everyone, including Billy Beelzebub, in the dust.

I am tired of hearing Franklin's playing, so by the time he goes on to close the evening, I am usually outside smoking a cigarette. It's not that I don't like the way Franklin plays. It's technically perfect. It's just that it has no heart, which is something I can't explain. And when music has no heart, it creates a vacuum in which no human emotion can exist. No joy, no sensuality, no hope. No pain, no loneliness, no grief. So when Franklin plays, I feel the walls closing in on me, and I feel the air being sucked out of the room, and I have to escape.

This particular night, while Franklin is playing and I'm outside smoking, Billy Beelzebub finds me.

He says, "You know, your boss doesn't encourage music."

I say, "Why should he? Why should anyone encourage music? If you can stop playing, you should."

Billy shrugs, taking the cigarette from me, and says, "Anyone who tries to keep music from the people is doing the devil's work."

I say, "A strange sentiment coming from someone whose last name is Beelzebub."

"That's just my stage name," he says.

I light another cigarette to replace the one he stole, and say, "Billy, that is not a name to mess around with."

"Aw, it's just for fun," he says, suddenly morphing into Hank Williams. "Besides, my music has a right to be heard, no matter what I'm calling myself."

I say, "If you spent as much time on your music as you do on your image and your grumbling, someone might encourage it."

He smirks, squinting at me as smoke curls around his eyes and gets trapped under the lip of his cowboy hat. "Is that how you talk to your students?"

"No. My students are there to learn, so I encourage them. You might want to think about signing up for lessons."

"I don't want to learn no fiddle," he says. Believe me when I tell you this man has learned everything he knows about the South from the movies. Those of us who actually survived an upbringing there don't suffer pretenders gladly. They don't know what they're wishing for. They don't understand the pain and tragedy and history of bloodshed that led to the superiority of its music. Such things don't come cheap.

I have a student, Joshua, a teenage boy who is being forced to learn violin, even though his real ambition is to play keyboards like Stevie Wonder. He goes to Crossroads, a rich white private school in Santa Monica, and his mother drives him to his lessons in their Jaguar. When she can't take him, she sends him in a limo. He tells me he never wanted to learn the violin (which was his mother's idea, of course) because it is such a white instrument. A rich white instrument at that, he says. "You don't understand," he told me. "I despise my pedigree. I'd give everything I have just to have been born black in East Compton."

I don't think I slapped him. I remember wanting to. In the old days I would have terrorized him with a barrage of words, which might have included "privileged pansy-assed ingrate." But these weren't the old days, so I think I said something like, "Be careful what you wish for."

"Oh," he said, puffing up his nonexistent chest, "or what? I might turn black? I hope God is listening."

I gently directed him back to his scales.

I thought he would stop showing up for lessons after that, but he didn't. His rebellion and his dreams of being black were encased in the cotton of privilege.

I am thinking of delivering the lost diatribe to Billy Beelzebub when the front door opens and Clive comes rushing out. His eyes are shining and he is a little winded.

He says, "Pearl, you gotta come hear this kid."

"What kid?"

"He just got up onstage with Franklin. Can't be more than fifteen. You've never heard anybody play harp like this."

I take the last drag off my cigarette, and I consider saying, Oh, who cares? Everyone plays the harmonica. But Clive is standing there with all this hopeful enthusiasm, and I know if I walk away I will just start to feel old.

I turn to Billy. "Shall we go hear the latest prodigy?"

Billy shakes his head. "No, man, my work here is done." And he lopes off into the night.

I follow Clive back into the performance room, and I can hear the harmonica blaring, hitting and bending and harmonizing notes as if powered by God's own breath. I am drawn to it, the way the children were drawn to the Pied Piper. We stand in the back of the room, and I watch this tall, lanky white kid wailing away on his harp while Franklin struggles to keep up with him on guitar. Franklin has a stiff, bewildered smile on his face. I can see his admiration for the kid, mixed with intense envy and a dash of frustration. Clive and I stand very still, just listening, watching. The audience is going nuts, or as nuts as any coffeehouse audience ever does, which means they are clapping and issuing forth the odd "Whoo!" and "Go ahead!"

When the song ends, the room erupts in applause, and even Franklin claps, smiling at the kid, who bows humbly toward his audience. Then Franklin bows, which is a tiny bit pathetic, as if he were part of the phenomenon. The kid tucks his harmonica into his pocket, gives a little wave, and leaves the stage.

Franklin says, "That's all we have tonight, folks. Come on out again next month."

Someone inquires after the kid's name. Franklin says, "Adam Pearce. That was Adam Pearce. Thanks, Adam."

Adam nods at Franklin. He is making his way to the door. Everyone wants to confront him, including Clive and me, but we all stand frozen, as if we haven't earned the right.

He walks right past a woman about my age. She is wearing jeans and a nylon jacket and battered Keds. She gives him a nod of admiration as he passes. He pauses, and glances over his shoulder at her, and she follows him.

It is his mother, I realize. And she had not asked for a piece of the pie. She brought him here so that he could have his moment. That was all.

"Pearl, what's wrong?" Clive asks, touching my shoulder.

"What?"

"Are you okay?"

I realize I am crying, in public, which is something I don't do.

For me, it all started in the second grade, when the class was auditioned for the school band. That was back in the day when there was such a thing as a music program in public schools. I had had no exposure to music before that. My parents didn't like it. Didn't even seem to trust it. My father was an ex-army guy and a genuinely humorless individual. He believed that life was all about sacrifice and hard work. He was the premier carpenter in the small town where we lived. A child of poverty, he had never really recovered from it. His own family had lived from handout to handout until his father, a part-time drunk, finally procured a position as a full-time grave digger. It was

73

excellent work for my grandfather. No one cared how much a grave digger drank, as long as he didn't actually fall into one of the holes, which grave diggers often did. Far as I know, my grandfather always managed to pass out aboveground, which kept him in good stead with his employer.

My father, to his credit, grew up with an intense dislike of alcohol. Never touched the stuff. Unfortunately, he associated alcohol with all other forms of pleasure, from music to literature, and so none of it was available to me. I went to school, and I went to the local Methodist church, which was where I first heard music. My father frowned on my efforts to sing along with the hymns. He said I should just be quiet and listen. So I did listen, with those wolf-like ears of mine, digesting and internalizing every note.

My mother didn't argue with him on this particular point, though she argued with him on every other point, it seemed. Their fights were loud and cruel, falling just short of violence. (My father was too proud to hit a woman, though the expression on his face told my mother and me that he was not entirely above it.) They called each other names. My mother broke dishes. My father slammed doors and sometimes drove off into the night. I didn't attempt to intervene, but after the storm had passed, I would sometimes ask my mother what it was all about.

My mother, a former department store model who was still quite beautiful, would sit in front of a vanity mirror perched on the kitchen table, wearing nothing but a slip and drinking iced tea and smoking as she pounded powder on her face.

It was always swelteringly hot in this memory. Our summers were hot, to be sure, and the kitchen was the center of the house. The windows were thrown open, and sometimes my mother would put a fan in front of a bucket of ice. Cheap man's airconditioning because we couldn't afford the real thing. It was the heat that made my mother particularly angry, but she always seemed to be mad about something much deeper. The heat was just an excuse.

"Your father believes women are slaves," she told me. "He believes they should be seen and not heard. Well, I am not going to live the life my mother did. My mother was a weak individual. She let my father get away with murder. My father hated me. He only cared about my brother. And did Mama ever defend me? No, she did not. She just served me up. She sold me down the river."

The fan whirred. The bucket of ice made no difference.

I had no idea what any of her talk meant. I only knew that my name was Pearl, and my grandmother's name was Pearl, and if my mother hated the original Pearl as much as she claimed to, what the hell was I doing lugging her name around?

"My family had money," my mother would tell me. "My father worked for the oil company. We never wanted for anything. Your father is just plain old white trash, but I am above that. I am not accustomed to living this way."

(She never identified which oil company, and I suspected it was just one of her stories. The grandfather I knew was a kind of jack-of-all-trades, one of those trades being a tobacco farm. If he was rich, I could never see evidence of how he got there. Or how any of us had benefited from it.)

"What way, Mama?" I asked. "What way are we living?"

"Poor," she spat out. "We are dirt poor. We live from one paycheck to the other. I can't even afford wall-to-wall carpeting like my friends have. I am not used to living like this."

"But Daddy works hard," I said.

I had no real evidence of this except that he left the house every morning in work clothes and came back, usually, after dark, talking about work.

"Ha! Works hard like a bum. He could own this town if he had a spine. Which he doesn't. He's a jellyfish. He's weak. Listen to me, Pearl, don't you ever marry a man like your father unless you want to suffer for the rest of your life."

"Okay, Mama."

"Your father says we can't afford air. He doesn't have to worry. He works in rich people's houses all day. Please don't hang on me, Pearl. You know how I hate the heat."

I was always trying to think of a way to make my mother proud of me. Outside of money, the only thing she seemed to value was accomplishment. She loved it when I got good grades. I hid the bad ones so she wouldn't have to cry. But there weren't many to hide. I was a good student. My first-grade teacher told Mama I was the smartest child she had ever taught.

"You hear that?" Mama said when she gave me the news. "You have the real ability to go places in the world. Don't throw it away."

I didn't want to throw it away. So when they auditioned us for the elementary school band, I decided to do my best. They brought the second graders in to listen to the fourth and fifth graders play. Then they gave us a sheet of paper and a pencil. Someone in the band played a note, and for every note after that, we were to make a mark if the subsequent note was higher or lower. I got all my answers right. I was the only one.

The bandleader, Mr. Compton, took me aside after the experiment and said, "Pearl, you have a real ear for music. You tell your mama that we want you in the school band. You pick whatever instrument you want to play."

I ran home from the bus stop, all excited, clutching the piece of paper in my hand. I found my mother, sitting in the kitchen with a glass of iced tea and a cigarette. I told her all about the experiment, how I was going to be in the band and I could pick my instrument.

She just stared at me as I talked, and she didn't smile, and I felt my voice getting smaller and smaller as her eyes narrowed.

"We can't afford that," she said.

"But I'm good," I told her. "Mr. Compton said I was the best."

"We can't afford it," she repeated.

"Afford what?"

"They'll make you pay for the instrument."

I thought about that for a moment, then said, "I have money. I've saved my allowance."

"No. We just can't afford it. And I don't have a car when your daddy is at work, so I can't pick you up if you have to stay for practice."

"Maybe I could pick a cheap instrument," I said.

"Pearl. We cannot afford it. You just concentrate on your studies."

She took a drag from her cigarette and blew the smoke into the stale air of the kitchen.

I am sure I am painting my mother in a harsher light than she deserves. The two of them, I later realized, were in a competition, and I was constantly being asked to choose. I didn't know how. My father was tall and handsome and knew how to build things with his hands, but as my mother often explained, he couldn't boil water. I knew you had to boil water to cook. My mother was a good cook. So siding with her meant I could live. Until something broke down in the house or a bill needed paying, because, my father explained, she didn't have the first clue about how things worked.

I realized they only worked well as a unit, so I devoted my childish efforts to keeping that unit together. It was my only hope of survival. I didn't know the first thing about dividing to conquer. I only knew about cobbling together the broken pieces and praying at night in my bed.

But what I also knew about God was that he was listening to everyone. And I was sure all the other prayers were competing with mine.

Two years later, when I was ten, I was playing at my friend Carolyn Millner's house. Her family had money, and the only reason I was let into that particular social circle was that I was a better student than Carolyn and I came over sometimes to help her study. Both my parents were thrilled with this connection because Carolyn's family was rich. One time when I was there, Carolyn was practicing the violin. I asked her to show me how to play.

She sighed and said, "Pearl, it's complicated."

"Just show me."

"No. I have to practice."

"How did you learn?" I asked her.

"My mother teaches me. She went to a music conservatory. She could have had a classical career. But she fell in love with my father."

"If you don't show me, I won't do your homework for you."

I did her English homework for her all the time. We pretended that I was helping, but really I was diagramming sentences for her. Carolyn's parents were aware of this but never objected. They just wanted her to get good grades.

So Carolyn spent an afternoon showing me how to make the notes and how to bow.

I caught on quickly, and soon it became part of her payment for my help on the homework. One time, her mother walked in and saw me playing. She was surprised and at least pretended to be delighted.

"Why, Pearl," she said, because she talked that way, "you have a natural ear."

"I was the best in my class," I informed her.

She chuckled and said, "You're holding the instrument all wrong, though. Your left hand should be curved. See, like this."

And she positioned my hand. Suddenly I could reach the notes much more easily. She must have seen the grateful look in my eye. She had blond hair and smelled of gardenias. My mother had black hair and smelled of something much sweeter. Her makeup was soft and quiet, not as thick and intrusive as my mother's. Up close, I could see that Carolyn's mother was what my mother was trying to be, and it made me sad.

Mrs. Millner said, "If you keep helping Carolyn with her studies, I'll teach you how to play."

I agreed. And I continued to help Carolyn, long after she had completely lost interest in me, other than to label me a freak among her friends. I didn't care how much Carolyn hated me. Her mother was teaching me to play the violin. When I turned thirteen, the Millners gave me my own instrument. When I brought it home, my mother said, "Take that back. We don't accept charity."

My father said, "For God's sake, Ella, let her keep it. She doesn't ask for much."

My mother looked at him and said, "I suppose that's what you admire in a woman. That she doesn't ask for much."

That was the last anyone in my house said on the matter. I was allowed to keep the violin.

And so my tragic infatuation was born.

5

I will tell you the truth. I don't live in an apartment anymore. When I moved out shortly after Roy disappeared, I was searching for something different. I was teaching Hallie then, and I had the misguided courage of one who thinks she's onto something. So I moved into a trailer park.

Few people realize those exist in Los Angeles County. This one is only a few blocks away from McCoy's, hidden between an industrial warehouse and a run-down neighborhood riddled with power lines. I don't live here to be cool or to make a point. I live here because I finally got fed up with apartment dwelling, got tired of smelling other people's food, their hideous concoctions of garlic and cheese, tired of hearing the droning of their overworked TVs and their fights and their perpetually cranky toddlers. None of which I would have minded had they been equally tolerant of my music.

But no, I had to endure their whiny complaints about my scales or my attempts at playing Mozart, even as they burped and farted their way through an evening of *Access Hollywood*.

I couldn't afford a house, and truth be told, there is no more privacy in a trailer than in an apartment, but at least the people here are accustomed to putting up with shit. No one expects privacy or politeness. (It is more reasonable to expect snow than politeness in Los Angeles.) We all simply ignore one another's noise. We accept that we have neighbors and that their business of living is going to look and sound slightly, or even greatly, different from our own, and that's just the price you pay for being poor in the land of excess.

My trailer is on the last row, away from Pico, backing onto the warehouse parking lot, so I have more privacy than most. I have to put up with the sounds of trucks pulling in at all hours of the day to unload whatever it is they store there. But I find that it neatly drowns out the high notes of my violin, and I actually enjoy trying to make a louder noise; sometimes I use the thumping of the truck engine as a bass line. There is music everywhere if you are willing to listen.

No one at McCoy's knows I live in a

trailer park. I'm not sure what they'd make of it, but it's not as if we visit one another in our off-hours. When we aren't working, we go off and live our imagined lives. The boys pretend to have torturous relationships with girls, and I pretend to go home and compose music, something I once actually did. I have sheets of songs stored away somewhere, sitting in file boxes, a veritable fire hazard in what should be my linen closet. I stopped trying to compose after Hallie. Now I watch peculiar specials on PBS or the Learning Channel, about the Underground Railroad, abnormal psychology, and the history of giants. I am learning things I never knew I was interested in.

This is what I'm doing when there is a knock on my door on an otherwise ordinary Wednesday. It is close to midnight. I am eating macaroni and cheese, drinking cheap chardonnay, and learning about code breaking at Bletchley Park in England during World War II. Because I don't expect it to be Franklin, I make no attempt to hide my pathetic existence. I expect it to be my next-door neighbor, Ralph, a fat and lonely bachelor who drops by at all hours under the pretense of borrowing a can opener, instead of several bottles of Bud, which I keep in the fridge just for him.

"I saw your light on," Franklin says, as though he were simply wandering in my neighborhood.

I am in sweats with my hair in a braid, holding my glass of cheap chardonnay, ready to say something sarcastic to Ralph. Instead I simply stare at Franklin, wondering where to start. Apologize for what first? My appearance, my trailer, the absence of a life? He seems genuinely uninterested in any of those.

I let him in, and he stands in the trailer for a moment, looking around as if he has suddenly found himself inside an Egyptian tomb. There is nothing particularly strange about my trailer, outside of its being a trailer. Inside, it looks like a studio apartment — a couch, which pulls out into a bed, facing a modest-sized television on an Ikea entertainment center, a coffee table, a bookshelf, a small kitchen table, an even smaller kitchen, a bathroom beyond that. I have pictures on the wall and flowers in a vase. I have a clock. I have a music stand. I have magazines.

"I got your address from our roster," he says, as if he has to explain.

"You thought it was an apartment, I'll bet."

He nods, still looking around, as if the

whole concept is going to go twirling off into the sky, like Dorothy's house in *The Wizard of Oz.* I flick off the television.

"Want a drink? I've got beer and wine."

He says he'll take a beer. He sits as I open it and pour it into a glass. I top up my wine and sit on a kitchen chair, a safe distance from him. Not because I think he'll attack me (I wish he would attack me), but because I'm afraid he'll see just how old and dry my skin is, how my breasts have started to travel south. But he's not looking at any of that.

He sips the beer, then says, "I'm glad you're awake. I've got stuff on my mind, and I wanted to talk."

"Good," I say. "I like stuff."

He takes a breath, scratches his head, and says, "I want to start a band."

"Oh." This isn't what I expected. The fact that I'm still expecting something speaks to a kind of desperation that I've yet to accept.

"It was playing with that kid, that harp player, Adam. Remember, the open mic?"

I nod.

He says, "I really enjoyed that. He just got up there and started wailing. First, I was irritated because it was my set. But then I saw my part in it. I support him, he supports me. I've never been good at being in a band because I don't like to share the spot-light."

I smile. "Oh, you're the musician who doesn't like to share."

He misses my humor. I'm used to it.

He says, "That's why I have always played alone. I always want it to be about me. I want my solo."

"You can have a solo in a band."

"Yeah, that's what I'm figuring out. But I never liked it before. I never liked the audi-ence. I guess that's what it is. A lot of how I play is just a trick, something I've learned and committed to memory. I lost respect every time the audience fell for it. But what happened with that kid? It was organic. It had a life of its own."

I light a cigarette without asking. I know Franklin hates smoking, but I figure he's in my house now. Or my trailer. Besides, something about his presence is irritating, and I want to push it away. Even so, I know that his being in my living room is a kind of turning point in both our lives. We are reaching out. We are chipping away at our isolation.

Franklin says, "When I heard the audi-ence respond to what we were doing, it's like a light went on in my head. They want to see something live. They want to see something evolve. It's a kind of magic. It's alchemy."

"Right."

He looks over at me. "Did you always know that?"

"Not always," I admit.

"You play in bands?"

"Not in a long time. Have you?"

"Not in years," he admits. "I've been focusing on other things."

"Like session work."

"Other things," he says deliberately. He doesn't want me to identify what those other things are. "What have you been doing instead?"

"Well, I was married for a long time."

"And that kept you from playing in bands?"

"Not in the beginning."

"He started to complain?"

He started to complain. I wasn't sure when it happened. It wasn't overnight. It was a gradual tension in the house when I practiced, and a sour mood when I came home from a gig. Later, he would be asleep with a note on the door for me not to wake him, to sleep downstairs. Eventually it became a fight. Like the one about my not taking his name. Evidence that I didn't love him enough, that I wasn't committed, that I wasn't putting the marriage first.

I believed him. I loved him. He thought that if I put the music down, I could love him more. As if it were another man diluting my attention. I didn't know what to think. Toward the end, I was just trying to prove something.

"When you did play, what kind of music was it?" he asks.

"All kinds. Mostly bluegrass."

"So you're not kidding about that."

"No."

"Do you like it?" he asks. "Playing in a group?"

"When it's going well, there's nothing like it."

"And when it's not going well?"

"There's something in that, too. But come on. You know all this."

"I have a Kryptonite," he says.

I nod. Most musicians are comic-book nerds.

"I hate messing up," he says.

"Everybody hates that."

"You ever mess up?"

"Of course."

"What did you do?"

"Come on," I say, feeling a little impatient. "You know the rule. People listen with their eyes. When you mess up, you just keep smiling and they never know."

"But you know," he says.

"Sure, I know."

"How do you live with it?"

I laugh.

"Isn't it humiliating?" he asks.

"I don't let humiliation in. Anymore."

"How did you get past it?"

"I just figure I'm trying something. I'm making an effort. It's easy to scoff when you aren't trying. The way I see it, the world is divided into two parts. People who do stuff, and people who mock the people who do stuff. I'd rather be a doer."

"I've never gotten past it," he says.

I nod, smoking my cigarette and inspecting him as I squint. He stares at me, waiting.

I say, "Music is like Communion or something. You don't do it because you're perfect. You do it because you glimpse perfection. You realize it can take you a step closer. You move toward it because you're hoping it can make you better."

Franklin nods and stares into the foam of his beer.

"Do you ever regret it? Regret the first time you heard a song you loved and wanted to make that sound? Be a part of it?"

"No."

"You don't? You don't wish you had been good at something else, like science or math?"

"Oh, that isn't scary? Calling Albert Einstein. Calling J. Robert Oppenheimer."

"Or cooking," he says, as if expecting that retort. "Or having babies."

"Botulism," I say. "Placental abruption. Being alive is scary, Franklin."

He takes a long, satisfied sip from his beer, as if this is exactly the conversation he wanted to have. I can see that I haven't disappointed him, and that makes me nervous, as if I have something to lose.

"I want to start a band," he says, coming full circle. "I want you to be in it."

"Okay," I answer.

"Just like that?"

"What else am I doing?"

He smiles. "A bluegrass band, I'm thinking. Well, more like a duo,"

"Okay, a bluegrass duo. You on guitar, me on fiddle. Who sings?"

"Me, probably," he says.

"Sure, why not."

"That's a real thing, a bluegrass duo, right?"

"Real as anything."

He laughs and says, "What will we call ourselves?"

"The Rogues," I suggest.

He shakes his head. "Too simple."

"The Trailer Park Rogues."

His smile is slow and long. Our eyes meet.

"Is that why you got divorced? Because of your music?" he asks.

"There's never one reason. So they tell you in counseling."

"But what do you think?"

"On my good days I think that. I chose it over the other thing. I couldn't live without it. I committed to the life of an artist."

"And the bad days?"

"He just fell out of love with me."

"Does that really happen?"

"I don't know."

"So this isn't a bad day."

"It's a neutral day. On the neutral days I try to think of something else."

"Like what?"

"Starting a bluegrass duo."

I stub my cigarette out and stand.

He stands, too. I know perfectly well that we could sleep together. I could move closer to him, I could let him kiss me. I could show him how the couch folds out. I could put some music on the stereo and light some candles. I could tell him to keep the noise down, and I could remind him that it doesn't mean he's obligated to me in any way. But I don't do that because I've done it before, and there is always the morning to contend with. The morning is an instrument out of tune, reminding you that it only sounds good if you pay attention to it.

Franklin pats me on the shoulder and leaves.

Hallie's adopted mother, Dorothy, started out hating music and soon came to love it. She found her place at McCoy's. She found an audience. She bonded with Franklin and Ernest, and even with Declan, who bonded with no one who didn't understand the basic construction of a stringed instrument. (She never really bonded with Patrick, but then, who does?) Dorothy always came in looking gloomy, but left with a kind of manic energy, which caused her to talk to me about things. I didn't want to talk about things, other than Hallie's progress. Hallie didn't know much about the mechanics of the violin when I first started teaching her, but she absorbed the information quickly, and I never had to nag her about how to hold the bow or about how to hit a note on the fingerboard. She played by ear, in the best possible way. The sounds circled around her, and she pulled them out of the air and brought them down. Then she lifted them on her strings and sent them back out into the atmosphere. This is how it happens. But it is hard to explain, and most students never really get it.

When Dorothy wrote me a check at the end of each month, she always said, "The money comes in from the state. My husband, Earl, deposits it. Sometimes I tell him, 'Look, if we could find a cheaper teacher, we could put some of that money in the bank.' But Earl, he's so honest. He's a deacon in the church. He doesn't want to know about cheating."

"Well, that's good. Government fraud isn't really the way to go."

"He lives for our boys. We have two boys. One, Hallie's age. Another two years older. We never expected to inherit another child."

Once, she leaned closer to me and said, "Do you think she's all right?"

"Hallie? She's fine. She's more than fine. She's very talented."

Dorothy nodded and said, "My sister made a big deal out of talent. She thought it was important. Is it?"

"Depends on who you ask," I told her.

But I knew what was going on. I saw that gleam starting in her eye, the same gleam that all the other parents who are pushing their children have, wanting to know if their child has "it." They aren't entirely sure what "it" is. Maybe it's a psychic ability. A supernatural gift. It can make a person crazy or it can make a person rich. It needs harnessing; it needs to be tamed. Ultimately, the question isn't what "it" is but where it is leading. And if it is leading to something good, the important thing, for the parents, once the gleam starts in their eye, is how to get some credit. Should they be hard or encouraging? Should they push or hang back? What gets their name in the liner notes or the memoirs?

The one thing I knew about talent was that it stirred people up. It threw them off balance. They wanted to shut it down or steal it. No one could look the other way in its presence. Dorothy was becoming no exception.

"What do you think?" Dorothy asked again.

"About talent? I don't entirely understand it myself. I just know that when you have it, there's a kind of moral obligation to own it and do something with it."

"And Hallie really has it?"

It. The stash of gold hidden in the mine, disguised as a surly adolescent.

"She has it," I admitted, though I immediately wished I hadn't. I knew it changed the way Dorothy saw her inherited daughter, and I knew it wasn't necessarily a good thing, for all the reasons I'd already considered. But since Dorothy treated Hallie as if she were worthless, I figured there might be an upside to giving the girl a face value.

Then I watched how Dorothy walked out with Hallie, a hand on her shoulder, as if she couldn't afford to let go of her, knowing what she knew now.

Hallie glanced back at me, I remember, with a look of accusation and dread. Thanks a lot, her expression said. The secret is out.

The secret is something that only musicians understand. Music does not come from us. It comes through us. It is a voice from beyond. It is the bridge between the logical world and whatever else exists. Of course, if you want to get scientific about it, it's nothing more than physics. A finite amount of energy, being pulled from the air and processed. When you play a musical instrument, you are simply converting energy from one form to another. But it doesn't feel like that. It feels as if you are picking up the voices of the ages, the screams or the prayers of the dying, the joy of the triumphant.

It's you and it isn't you. But how can that

be? How can there be something greater than you and the instrument working together? How can there be a third thing that comes to life just because you've drawn a bow across some strings? It's the mystery of the Trinity. How can there be three Gods and only one?

How it can be ceases to matter at some point. It only is, and that is the secret. That is the "it." Alchemy. Spinning all the parts into gold. This is what makes an artist run to church or into a bottle or a river. It was what made Michelangelo pound the knee of his *Moses* and demand it to speak. It cannot be, but it is, and there is so much more of it than we can understand. And then, once we've glimpsed it, they expect us to walk around in the world with everyone else. Go to the car wash and the grocery store and sign up for normal, for the mundane ugliness of the world in front of our eyes.

This is the thing you stop talking about early on, but it haunts you, this knowing that there is something beyond you and your hapless plans and that it has picked you out as its messenger. Like Mary in the manger, you keep all these things and ponder them in your heart. Mary said yes to her assignment. But most of us say maybe. Which is worse than no.

I certainly never told Hallie any of this. Not because she wouldn't have understood. But because she would have understood completely.

That was the last normal session with Hallie, the last time before I started to know other things. Once you learn something, you can't unlearn it. Once you hear a tune, you are stuck with it forever.

6

Franklin puts a sign up on the wall inside McCoy's. It says, THE TRAILER PARK ROGUES — A BLUEGRASS DUO. AVAILABLE FOR BOOKING. He takes an enormous amount of teasing about it, but Franklin is strangely unaffected by the comments of his peers at work. He resists telling them I'm in the band, too. He says, "Look, we're a duo and we're available for booking." Clive wants in, but Franklin says no. "Stand-up bass only," Franklin says. "We're bluegrass and that means pure instruments." Clive says he can do that. Franklin just keeps saying no.

A day later, another sign goes up next to that one. It says, YES, WE HAVE SITARS! I stare at it for a long time, as if it were a puzzle, until I realize who put it there. The Puzzle himself.

"People like sitars," Patrick tells me.

"But they're like guns," I say. "Nobody

should get near one unless they know how to use it."

"George Harrison knew how to use it," he tells me. For the first time, I'm surprised to admit, I realize that Patrick has a slight lisp. It's not so much a lisp as an inability to pronounce *s*'s. They collect in the back of his throat and hiss, emerging as a kind of *sh* sound. "George Harrishon knew how to ushe it." How did I miss this about Patrick? Because he doesn't talk much, I figure.

"Is that your instrument?" I ask him. "The sitar?"

"I don't have an instrument, Pearl," he says. "Which is to say, I don't attempt to claim one."

I don't push it again, but he has to have an instrument. Franklin insists on knowing a person's instrument before he hires him. Maybe Patrick lied on his application. Which has to be around somewhere, in our files. I tell myself to do some research on Patrick's day off. I'm not sure why I want to know. I just want to know.

At the end of several days, there still aren't any takers for our duo. Franklin comes to me with the sad news. He wants to disband already. I say to him, "Franklin, give it more than a month. Are you so afraid of failure you can't even try?"

"Yes!" he says emphatically. "I'm that afraid of failure. Why aren't you?"

"Failure has just never impressed me. That's all. It seems like a temporary condition."

Franklin leaves the sign up on the wall.

At the end of the week, there are still no takers, and Franklin is truly despondent. He has also called every booker in town, and while they know him and respect him, they say that a bluegrass duo simply isn't a draw these days.

"What are we going to do?" he asks me one night as he's counting the money in the cash register and I'm filing receipts. "I thought it was the answer to my restlessness. I thought it was going to cure me."

"Well, we could play an open mic somewhere."

"You're kidding," he says with a look of disgust. For him, for most serious musicians, this is like a Shakespearean actor consenting to do a diarrhea commercial.

"Well, think about it. I mean, what if someone hired us? We don't know any songs. We've never played together," I say.

"If someone hired us, we'd learn some. We'd throw something together."

"So let's throw something together and play an open mic. Let's do some Ralph

Stanley songs. Or the Carter Family. I could teach you."

He smirks. "I know those songs."

"So let's play an open mic, just for practice. There's a good one in Venice, a place called the Cow's End."

He raises an eyebrow. "Is it a bar?"

"Coffeeshop."

"Oh, for God's sake." He looks as if he might vomit. "Trying to play over the sound of a cappuccino machine?"

"Starting at the bottom is half the fun," I tell him.

"Yeah? What's the other half?"

"I don't know yet."

He sighs, blowing the beleaguered breath through his lips. "All right. You do the research. Tell me when and where."

I say, "While we're at it, doing research, what instrument does Patrick play?"

He looks at me. "You don't know?"

"No. Do you?"

He thinks about it, his eyes roaming across the cork ceiling. "Horns?"

I shrug. "That could be it."

We don't have any horns to speak of at McCoy's, unless you count recorders, so he could keep that particular talent hidden well enough.

But then Franklin says, "I don't think it's horns."

"Piano?"

"God, no," Franklin says. He has an irrational distrust of the piano, for reasons he can't sufficiently explain.

"If he's good at something, he could be in our band," I suggest.

"No," he says emphatically. "The band is you and me. Period. The whole point is that I can only start small. Two people is all I can handle right now. If it works, we can build."

"Okay." I relent, a little flattered by his insistence. "But he does play an instrument? You're the one who thinks he's a theory nerd."

"I do think he's a theory nerd, but he has to play something. I'm sure he told me when I hired him. I can't remember."

He continues to count the money, his guitar-callused fingers flipping through the bills. After a moment he looks up and says, "I'm still thinking about dumping Clive."

"Still? Why?"

"I don't know why. I don't trust him."

"Is he stealing?"

"No, of course not," he says, finishing up with his efforts and putting the money into a locked safe. "I just don't trust bass players."

"Why the hell not?"

He shrugs. "They aren't trustworthy."

"They hold the beat," I say.

He rolls his eyes. "They think they do."

"But they do. They are the last line of communication between the guitar and the drums. Singers rely on them. They are important."

"They have an elevated sense of themselves."

"Maybe they're right to."

"They are always trying to take over the universe," he tells me.

"Well, the bottom end is the spine of music."

"Spine my ass," he says, and I laugh, knowing full well that he misses the humor.

He says, "Where's the bottom end in bluegrass? I'll tell you where. In the guitar. It's the only place they use the guitar as a percussion instrument, which is what it is."

I smile. "Why all this sudden passion for bluegrass, Franklin?"

"It's not sudden. You know that. You know it's my discipline. It's the purest kind of music," he says. "Outside of the blues. You know that."

"It's the hardest kind of music," I say.

"Outside of classical and jazz. To you, music is an intellectual pursuit."

"What's wrong with that?"

"Nothing. Except that music isn't really a thinking game. It's a feeling game."

"It's not a game at all," he says. "It's a profession."

"Fine," I say, surrendering.

He stares at the stained industrial carpet for a moment, then says, "You're the one who says bluegrass is about God."

"Yes, that's my argument. What's yours?"

Franklin looks at me until he can't. Then he stares at the wall, where dozens of beautiful guitars hang like icons. He says, "I'm pretty sure Patrick plays a horn. Saxophone, maybe. Or trumpet."

"Trumpet? Really?"

The trumpet, in my book, may be the only truly impossible instrument to play. Franklin must think so, too, or he wouldn't suddenly look so lonely and afraid. To be anything but the best is Franklin's gravest fear. I think I've always known that about him. I think I've always loved it, too.

I look at people's wrists. I do it out of habit. The wrist is all-important in violin playing, in any kind of stringed instrument, I suppose. But in violin, it is the foundation of the vibrato, which is the highest skill you can acquire. The right wrist has one function: to remain supple. But the left wrist, the one in charge of the fingerboard, has to be in equal parts strong and flexible. It's like yoga, I'm told. (In California, you are exposed to yoga against your will. It's everywhere, like smog. Even my fat, drunken neighbor Ralph does yoga. He says it keeps him aware. Aware of what? I want to ask. But I don't.) The left wrist has to be strong enough to hold the note but flexible enough to vibrate it. It's not for sissies. In fact, this is the point where most of my students drop out — when I start examining the spirituality of their wrists.

Most people's wrists are wasted aspects of their anatomy. I see it all the time. People (women especially) adorn their wrists with stupid things. Bracelets full of sparkling crap, or expensive watches that, because of their magnetic nature, actually inhibit the ability of the wrist to do its job. What is the job of the wrist? To bend and flex, then hold steady, then bend and flex again. Think of life without your wrist. You couldn't open a jar, turn on a bath tap, steer a car, turn up the volume. You couldn't wipe the sweat from your brow, or fan yourself, or type, or turn on the stove, or build a sandcastle, or tousle someone's hair. You couldn't throw a punch or shoot a gun. You couldn't blow a kiss. All this fuss is made over the opposable thumb. But really, it's the flexible wrist that makes human existence bearable.

Get me started on bracelets and watches, why don't you. I will identify them as man's last attempt to keep women down. (Long fingernails were a nice try, too. You can't do anything with long fingernails except paint them.) I discourage any sort of adornment there. I give my students wrist exercises. I make them walk around the house, holding their wrists limp, then flexing them at a ninety-degree angle. Strong wrist, strong future. Weak wrist, weak future. I say these things without irony.

You see, in violin playing, as I think I've mentioned, it's all about the bow. Just as with a stove, the gas might be turned on for hours, but until you light a match, nothing happens. The bow is the match. It ignites the sound. Sometimes — often, in fact — the student gets all hung up about the fingerboard, finding the note, finding the vibrato. But the bow is the living part of the instrument. The bow unleashes all the secrets. If the bow is stifled, music simply cannot be found. And bowing is all in the wrist.

So I saw the marks that day, when I was teaching Hallie. We were four months into lessons, and she was doing quite well. I had her playing some Bach sonatas. She breezed through the notation as if it were written in baby language. Her left hand moved effortlessly through the motions, her wrist curling and extending, finding the vibrato. But her right wrist, which controlled the bow, was stiff and frightened. I touched her there, to make a point. She screamed.

"What?" I asked as she backed away from me, tucking her instrument under her arm.

"You scared me," was all she said.

"I just want you to loosen your right wrist," I told her.

"I will," she said. "Just don't touch me."

"It would help if you would take off that bracelet," I informed her.

She just looked at me, and in that moment I realized that she wasn't wearing a bracelet. She realized that I had realized it. She backed away from me.

"Let me see it," I said.

She hesitated for a moment, but when she saw I was going to reach for her wrist, she offered it to me. I sucked in a breath as it came into focus. The whole thing was purple. But there were specific indentations, the size of fingertips, going all the way around it.

"What happened?" I asked.

"I caught it in the car door," she said evenly.

I lifted her arm into the light. This was not a car door injury. Her wrist had been grabbed and squeezed. The marks were as clear as a tattoo.

"Who did this?" I asked her.

She avoided my eyes.

"Hallie, tell me. I'm just going to ask your mother."

"She's not my mother," Hallie quickly informed me.

"All right. But who did this? Dorothy?"

She shook her head, then lifted her sad, doelike eyes to me. "I have brothers."

"Which brother did this?"

"Brian," she said. "He's almost sixteen. He's very strong."

"Why did he grab your wrist?"

"He didn't. That is, he didn't mean to. We were wrestling."

I tried to think of what to say. Finally I came up with this: "Doesn't he understand how important your wrists are?"

"He's a man. He doesn't understand anything," she told me.

I sat down in my metal folding chair and contemplated her life. She saw me doing it and sat down as well.

"It's not Christopher. He's only my age. He doesn't even talk to me. He thinks I'm weird."

"If you're getting hurt," I said slowly, "I have to tell someone."

"I'm not getting hurt," she assured me.

"But look at your wrist!"

"We were wrestling!"

I looked at her. I thought of her house. Her strange, angry adopted parents and their strange, confused boys, trying to adjust to an unwanted, unexpected girl. Someone was grabbing her around the wrist and bruising it. I didn't really care who it was or why.

"I think I'll have to talk to Dorothy," I said.

"No," she said, quickly, desperately. "You can't tell her."

"Why not?"

"She loves them more than me. She'll kick me out."

"She can't do that. She won't. Besides, I've talked to her. She's quite fond of you." I wasn't sure this was true, but I hoped it was.

She has recognized "it," I wanted to tell her. She knows there's gold in the hills.

Hallie looked away from me. "The family

is all in place," she said. "They're a unit. They have church and everything. I'm an intrusion. Is that the right word?"

"I guess," I said.

"If I'm trouble, they'll make me leave. I have nowhere else to go."

"They can't hurt you. It's not allowed."

"No one is hurting me," she said in a high, desperate tone.

Then she looked up at me with her sad, dark eyes, a look that was not so unlike Franklin's worried gaze. "They'll make me stop playing music. I can't stop playing music. I can't."

This was a far cry from her original incantation: "You can't make me play. I won't let you." I couldn't decide if this was progress or regression or something in the middle, like guidance.

"No one can take music away from you," I said in my institutional teacher's voice.

And then she looked at me with a maturity I did not recognize in myself, let alone in my students. Her face was pale and as still as granite.

"Of course they can take it away," she said. "They want to and they will. You know that. You know it's always a breath away from being gone."

"No, Hallie, I don't know that. You have

an ability. An understanding. No one can take that away. And this is unrelated to music. This is about you being hurt."

"I'm not being hurt," she said.

She swiveled her body away from me in her folding chair. She held the violin next to her chest as if it were a baby that needed comforting.

I said, "Look, I'm a teacher. I'm a mandated reporter."

"I don't know what that means."

"It means that if I see someone being hurt, I'm obligated to tell."

She lifted her head. "Tell who?"

"People who care about things like this."

She laughed. "Who the hell are those people?"

I was stretching the truth a little because I was only a music teacher. We weren't officially mandated reporters like public school teachers. But I suspected that if I went to some kind of authority, they would listen.

I said, "Hallie, the world isn't as indifferent as it seems. There are people who care about children."

Her eyes grew sad when I said this.

"I'm not a child," she told me, as if telling me she weren't a person.

"You are."

"Let's not talk about it anymore, okay? If you're someone who turns people in to authorities, I don't think I can come here anymore. Because you sold yourself to me as someone who doesn't believe in authority."

"I did? How did I do that?"

"You're a music teacher. That's not about authority. What we do in here, it's just about music."

"Music can't make you safe."

"Of course it can," she said. She lifted her violin to her chin. "Let's keep going."

We finished the lesson. I said nothing to Dorothy. The next week, the bruises had faded, and then there was nothing but alabaster skin. Her wrists grew strong, her bowing excelled, and I allowed myself to be lulled by the music, the eternal Pied Piper, until nothing else mattered but the sound of notes and chords and tones, drifting on the air like smoke from the chimney of the Vatican.

7

It's on a Friday evening, when I'm in charge of locking up the store, that I figure out the real reason Franklin wants to fire Clive.

My last student is late, so I'm half an hour behind, and it being a Friday, I'm eager to get out. Not because I have any special plans — it's been a while since I've taken any orchestra or session work, and much longer since I've had any kind of social life to attend to. I'm just tired of being at Mc-Coy's, and I'm feeling a little cranky after a conversation I had with my ex-husband earlier in the day. He called me at the store to give me some good news and some bad news. He said, "Stephanie's pregnant, and I'm not sure I can keep paying for your car."

I let a cold moment of silence go past before I said, "Where's the good news?"

"Stephanie's pregnant," he repeats.

"And who is that good news for?"

"Pearl, don't do this. You knew we were trying."

"I knew Stephanie was trying. You said you weren't interested. Or did I dream that?"

"Well, it's too late now, and I'll get happy about it eventually."

"Are you going to marry her?"

"Maybe. I don't know. The point is, I have to start saving money."

"How far along is she?"

"Two months," he says.

I stop myself from saying the very mean thing. It's early yet. Anything can happen. Clearly he has forgotten both of my miscarriages, one at ten weeks, one at fourteen. Maybe Stephanie's uterus is stronger than mine. Maybe he loves her more than he ever loved me. But I can't think about that. I have to focus on the possibility that she will encounter some kind of misfortune, that she won't just move in and take over my life and do all the things I couldn't do, such as keeping him interested. I'm pretty sure it's okay for me to want bad things to happen to her. But if I want bad things to happen to her unborn child, that might be crossing a line. I try to stop just short of being a bad person. It's harder than it sounds.

So instead of the very mean thing, I said

the sort of mean thing: "Will Stephanie have to give up her work in telemarketing?"

"Pearl, don't be this way. We don't have any formal financial arrangement. I was paying for your car as a favor."

"I see. And I suppose I didn't ask for alimony as a favor. If all favors are off now, perhaps I should get a lawyer."

Which is a hollow threat, because once you waive alimony, there's no going back. Not to mention that I can't afford a lawyer.

Mark says, "Look, the car is almost paid off. You'll just have to pick up the insurance payments. You might have to do a little more moonlighting, pick up some extra students. Is that really the end of the world?"

No, it wasn't really the end of the world. Nor is it the end of the world when the man you love starts looking at you like you're a stain on the carpet and shortly after that starts sleeping with a college student.

The world doesn't end, ever, apparently, despite all the warnings to the contrary. And that might be the bad news.

Probably what's bothering me is that the world isn't ending or even standing still. It keeps going with things like Stephanie's getting pregnant and my having to pay for my car, and that means I'm going to have to keep going with it.

So I told him to stop the car payments, of course, stop the insurance payments, I'd get by somehow. In the end I was gracious, even congratulated him on his progeny, wished him well, and then hung up. I got out of the call before I revealed my truest fear, which was that the car payment was the only real connection I still had to him, and that now he would go away forever, and that it might be the best thing for me, and that I might have to let go of this long-held resentment, and that this long-held resentment was what kept me interested.

I didn't love him anymore. I didn't. I didn't because I told myself I didn't, daily, when I brushed my teeth and drank my orange juice and warmed up my scales.

Now I would have to find something else to engage me. Maybe it would be the Trailer Park Rogues.

All of this is going through my mind as I'm closing up the store, so it takes me a while to realize that Clive is still hovering nearby, pretending to arrange guitar straps on the wall. I know he has clocked out because I checked all the time cards as part of my closing-up duty. I say, "Clive, what are you still doing here?"

He grins at me. Clive is from Los Angeles, which is something that almost no one is, except for people his age. The Los Angele-nos of his generation have names like Clive and Harry and Gerard and Simon, names that the rest of the country left behind in England, along with stiff social mores and colonial rule. Like most musicians of his generation, he tried a stint back east before figuring out that it is cold and unfriendly to Californians. Most places on earth are cold and unfriendly to Californians, as one of Joni Mitchell's better songs taught us. (She was actually from Saskatchewan, Canada, which also no one is.) I played that song for him once, and I saw his eyes fill up with awareness. That's why he always compares me to Joni Mitchell, because I played her songs for him and now he thinks we are one and the same.

Like most native Californians, he is baby-faced and scrubbed, his hair is naturally blond, though he has dyed it black (the blond roots peek through defiantly), and he has too many earrings in both ears, which suggests that he is actually too chicken to pierce anything else. I like that in a person.

In answer to my question, he says, "I'll walk you to your car."

"My car is right out front."

"Still, you shouldn't be here alone. With all that money and stuff. It's not safe."

I am about to remind him that Franklin will walk me to my car, which he usually does, but tonight he is not here. Clive reads my thoughts and says, "Franklin took off early. Maybe he has a gig somewhere, with that new band of his."

"No," I say. "That's impossible."

"Why?"

"Because I'm in that band of his."

"Oh, really? Can you get me in it, too?"

"No."

"Why not?"

"I don't know. Ask Franklin."

He shrugs, looks at his fingernails. "Franklin doesn't like me."

"That's not true," I say automatically, even though I know he is fixated on firing Clive.

Clive, who is smarter than anyone gives him credit for, says, "He doesn't like bass players. That's pretty common."

"He can't dislike you because of your instrument. You're good at it. That's why he hired you. You have more students than I do."

"More than Ernest, too."

"And more than Patrick."

"Who doesn't have any."

"That's because he doesn't play an instrument," I say.

"Sure, he does," Clive says.

"Oh? Which one?"

Clive thinks about it, then says, "I don't know, but he must play one. He knows so much about music. Listen to him talk."

"Franklin thinks he's a theory nerd."

"You can't learn about music from theory. You have to play," Clive informs me, as if I don't know that.

"Well, no one can identify his instrument. If you want to take that on as your mission, then go with God."

He shrugs again, stuffing his hands into his jeans pockets. "I just want to walk you to your car."

"Fine," I say. "Walk me."

We take about ten steps outside the door, him lugging his bass, me carrying my violin.

When we get to my car, I get mad all over again, thinking of my conversation with Mark. Suddenly I don't want to touch the car anymore. We used to ride around in it. We used to take it up the coast, to Malibu, for picnics, hanging out on the beach until the sun started to set. Then we'd find a dive bar and drink to the point where one of us still felt safe to drive, and then we'd go home. No more. No more.

As I'm putting my violin in the trunk, Clive says, "Listen, I want to take you to dinner."

I slam the trunk shut, then look at him.

"Why?" I ask.

He shrugs.

"You mean tonight?" I ask.

"No. Some other time."

I think about it for a split second.

"You're asking me on a date?"

He grins.

The smile comes before I can fight it, and I say, "Oh, Clive, this is so misguided."

"I like older women," he announces proudly.

"But I'm too much older," I say, not even bothering to do the math. But in no time, I've already played the scene out in my head. We have dinner in a cheap Italian restaurant, we drink too much wine, he takes me back to my trailer, he thinks the trailer is cool, he thinks I'm fantastic, I put on some Joni Mitchell, he likes me even more, I don't mind kissing him, I don't mind his hands on my breasts, I'm not afraid to be naked, I'm telling him what to do, he does it just fine.

And then the morning. Always the morning.

And then I'm pregnant. I'm pregnant! I call Mark and say, Guess who else is having a baby? and he is wild with jealousy, and he agrees to keep paying for my car, and in fact, he wants to talk to me, wants to tell me how stupid Stephanie is, how he wishes that he and I were having a baby together, and he asks me, How did this ever happen? And I tell Clive I'm pregnant, and he gets scared and dumps me, and then I tell Franklin I'm pregnant and I have to drop out of the band, and he falls in love with me because another man has gotten me knocked up, and then he agrees to raise the baby, and he forgets about the bluegrass band and session work and McCoy's and he gets a real job with his MBA and the baby comes.

And then he looks at me as if I'm a stain on the carpet.

Clive says, "Listen, I'll tell you a secret about me."

"Don't."

He says, "My first lover was my high school English teacher. She was fifteen years older than I was. It didn't last long. Then I dated girls my age. But the pattern is set, you know? It's like playing the bass. It's the rhythm. The rhythm exists in your head. You hear it and you play it. You don't ask why."

I say, "Only children don't ask why."

He looks wounded when I say this. Good,

I think. Good.

"Go home," I tell him. "Look in the mirror. Remember who you are. And that relationship was a mistake. The first one often is. The first one is just a matter of exploring your dark side."

He has lost interest in fighting me. Now he just wants to know what I mean.

"What was your first relationship?"

My first relationship. It ended in marriage.

"It was a mistake," I tell him. "I've been trying to escape it ever since."

Now he is standing on the sidewalk, looking like a little boy, much as he must have looked to his high school English teacher, who saw the bait and took it. She was a vampire. She was a thief. He is not ready to hear that.

I have to leave him with some dignity, so I say, "Thank you for asking. It is very flattering, but even if you were the right age for me, I'm not dating right now."

"Well, all right. But why? Why aren't you dating?"

"Because I'm still married," I tell him.

He seems surprised. "I thought you were divorced."

"On paper," I say.

He seems to hear this. Then he gives me a noncommittal wave and walks off down the street, his electric bass in a gig bag, bumping against his hip.

And I smile, in spite of everything, because of everything. Because I know now that Franklin saw this coming, and he wanted to head it off at the pass. Franklin wants me to himself.

It is the good news and the bad news.

When I was sixteen, Carolyn Millner's mother stopped teaching me violin. She had to. Carolyn was fully entrenched as a popular girl by then, and she simply couldn't tolerate me in her house. She told her mother this several times before it sunk in. Mrs. Millner loved me and loved teaching me, because she had glimpsed my talent, and true musicians always enjoy setting that thing loose from its cage. But in the end, a mother is always going to choose her daughter.

By then, I knew enough about technique, and I played music by ear, so I took my violin home and started teaching myself the rest. It drove my father crazy, hearing the scratchy scales coming out of my room, enduring my experiments with vibrato, listening to a single composition played a dozen and a half times.

Partly it was because the sounds in my

room wounded his ears. But it was also because he was a churchgoing man, and when my music sounded right, he knew, on some level, that I had invited God into my own little microcosm and that he, my father, was losing his grip on me. I was sixteen and on the verge of losing him altogether. He was, or claimed to be, a devout Christian, and his sole purpose in life by the time I grew breasts was to keep me away from men. He knew I couldn't actually love Mozart, a man with a ponytail who was long dead, but he heard me loving him, anyway, and it drove him crazy.

This was somewhere in the South in the 1970s. The war was grinding to a halt, Nixon was leaving, nuclear missiles were poised and ready to fly, the civil rights movement was under way and gaining ground. It was all too much for a simple man. My father prided himself on being simple, but a truer description was that he was elemental. He couldn't trust what he didn't understand, and he didn't understand much. There wasn't much left in his control, but he could be damn certain that I wasn't having sex.

I wasn't having sex. That fact was not enough for him.

He came to my room one night and said,

126

"All a poor girl has is her reputation."

I said, defiantly (and not really understanding my history, which is where defiance comes from), "We're not poor."

He said, "If I see you running around with boys, I will put a stop to it."

I thought he meant boys. He really meant music.

I started listening to Led Zeppelin and Bruce Springsteen, playing along with their violin parts. I also started wearing short cutoffs in the summer. My hormones were all over the place. So were my breasts.

I started making out with Johnny Pitt in the backseat of his Mustang. He knew how to kiss, and he found my breasts and gently pinched my nipples between his thumb and forefinger. It was enough for me. I started wearing colored mascara and Baby Soft perfume.

One night, my father came to my room and said, "Your mother and I are losing control of you."

I was sitting on my eggshell-colored carpet, looking at the album cover of the Rolling Stones' *Goats Head Soup.* There was a song on the record called "Dancing with Mr. D," and another that everybody called "Starfucker." The world was opening up before me like a flower.

I said nothing.

He said, "I am taking your violin away."

I shrugged. "Take it," I said.

He did.

I didn't object. I had lost interest in it. I was more interested in what Keith Richards did with a guitar and what Johnny Pitt did with my breasts.

After he took my violin, he took my records. I never knew what became of the records. I started listening to the radio.

We lived in this old Victorian mansion on the main street of a small town. The sound traveled quickly through the house and almost as quickly through the town. He took my stereo away. Then I was left with my transistor radio. Which was where I heard all the best music, on AM stations from places as far away as Chicago. I heard Lou Reed and Mountain and Todd Rundgren and MC5 and the entire world of Motown. I heard Al Green and Smokey Robinson and Marvin Gaye. Marvin Gaye was the best. Marvin Gaye did what Johnny Pitt wasn't brave enough to do. And when I heard my father pacing outside my room, I knew that he was aware of what was happening in there. I wasn't just having sex. I was having sex with a black man.

By the time I was seventeen, I had lost my

virginity, not in the way I had imagined, not in the way I had hoped, but to a boring prep school student in town, who was destined for greatness but wanted a taste of trash before he moved on. My mother knew it was happening. I never told her, but she knew. His name was Shreve Carter. His parents had money. My mother thought I might get some of it. My father knew I was being used.

I came home from school one day, my senior year, to find my father raking leaves in the backyard. My mother was gone. Shopping for groceries, he said. He never told me why he was home from work so early. He was just raking leaves. There were several small fires in the yard. It was legal to burn leaves in your yard in those days.

I walked out and stood beside him, inhaling the dangerously beautiful smell of the end of fall, the end of spring, the end of everything. It was a curious aspect of my personality that I preferred endings to beginnings. One of the fires was burning brighter than the others. I walked over to it and peered down. At the center of the pile of leaves was my beautiful violin, burning up, wilting and shriveling in the heat.

I almost wanted to grab it. But I didn't. I had let it go. I had abandoned it. I looked at my father.

He said, "I guess that will teach you."

It did, and it didn't.

I walk into my trailer and sit down on my couch. I pick up a magazine and toss it away. I pick up the TV remote control and toss that away, too. I take my violin out of its case. I stare at it. I have never felt safe enough to love it, not since the day I saw its sister, its cousin, its distant relative, being burned at the stake.

I could be having sex with Clive right now, I think.

I don't want sex, I remind myself. I want the other thing.

Some other thing.

I have never been able to define the other thing. It nags at me and scratches at the door like a stray cat. Sometimes I think it is God, but God wouldn't grovel, I figure. God wouldn't scratch at the door. Still, there has always been a voice nagging at me, telling me to pick up an instrument and play. It can't be my conscience. It can't be my ego. It is something against my will, begging for a song.

Sometimes, in a desperate moment, I think it is a phantom audience, a collection of ghosts, asking me to remind them of the virtue of being alive. If you are chosen to play music, you can hardly stop yourself from identifying with the Pied Piper. The Pied Piper, who rid a town of deadly rats, was not paid for his services, so in order to exact revenge, he led all the children away from the town, hypnotizing them with his beautiful music. I always understood that story. The people failed to see his magic, so he used his magic against them. And the fact that he used it on their children seems particularly fitting. The children wanted to go. Like musicians, they were misunderstood. They were looking for a way out.

The problem is, the Pied Piper never surrendered his flute. He knew it was his weapon. Without it, he would have been powerless.

My violin disappeared in a matter of minutes. I watched it dissolve until it blended with the leaves. Only the strings remained. They looked like scary, long fingernails. They curled on the ends. As they curled, they made a sound. They made music, even in death.

My father paid for me to go to a second-rate college. I studied journalism. I learned how to write. I was broken; I was burned, like the instrument. I carried around this guilt, knowing that my abandonment of the violin resulted in its death, same as if I had put a baby in a Dumpster.

But when I was a junior in college, I realized I had to fulfill a music requirement. I took a violin class. I had to. They made me. After the third class, my teacher said, "I can't do anything more with you. You are better than I am. You need to play with an orchestra or a band."

So I did. So I was back. My father was sick by then. He couldn't stop me. He had done his best.

It was too late by then, anyway. The secret was out. You can't kill music. You can only hide it. But it will be found. It lives to be found.

Maybe this was what my father was always trying to tell me: Once you find it, you are a slave to it forever. You serve it; it doesn't serve you. You can no longer pretend to be the master of your universe. As I sit alone in my trailer, realizing that I could be having sex, I let myself consider this possibility: that my father always knew sex was a weak substitute. Sex is dangerous, sex distracts, sex kills. But unlike music, it cannot disarm you. It cannot own you. He was asking me to choose between the lesser of two evils, or perhaps the weaker of two masters.

In any case, he succeeded. Because now I

am alone in a trailer park, without a man, without a cat, staring at an instrument I'm afraid to touch.

8

The following Monday, Franklin and I play an open mic at the Cow's End in Venice. It's a hip coffeeshop on a hip street near the Venice pier. The space is nice, even though we have to play on a glorified balcony, and the acoustics are good, which is the only thing a true musician cares about. There aren't many performers signed up that night, so we get to play four songs. We play a couple of Ralph Stanley numbers, a Doc Watson number, and, just for fun, a Who song, "Won't Get Fooled Again." Franklin is at the top of his game. He's even singing well. (I sing better, but I refuse to make him aware of it.) I play the part of the obedient backup musician. I use my violin to augment what he's doing. I sing harmony on some of the verses. Mainly I hang back and let him take center stage. I have never minded that. Violinists learn to do it over time. Women learn to do it long before that.

The secret to being a woman is hiding your smarts. You keep your mouth shut. You're patient. You wait. As far as I can tell, men and women are engaged in a kind of guerilla warfare. The first rule of guerilla warfare is that you use your enemy's weapons against him. If he lobs a bomb at you and it doesn't explode, you collect the bomb, fix it, and lob it back.

I decide not to lob any bombs this night, even though I could have done so in the form of some harrowing violin solo. I support his small and obvious goal because I have a bigger one in mind. I'm going to make him fall further in love with me. Then, when he's hooked, I'm going to tell him all about his obligation to get a real job with his MBA, and when he does, I'm going to be a professional musician.

Is this an evil plan or a good one? It's always so hard to tell. God and the devil wear each other's clothes.

In any case, when our set is over, we are the toast of the open mic. Several musicians come up to tell us how good we are. A young woman with bright red hair and an expensive guitar informs Franklin that she has a band and a manager, and they are looking for a great guitar player like him. Instead of saying, Fuck off, I'm already in a duo, and I wouldn't even be here if it weren't for my violin player, he smiles and nods and writes his phone number down on a scrap of paper. I stand off to the side and smile. I am waiting.

Franklin is practically drunk with praise by the time we leave. We are hungry and we walk down the street until we find a cheap Italian place that's still open. We order spaghetti and red wine, and I listen to him talk. He is full of talk, and I want to hear it all. I am patient.

He says, "Do you see? Do you see how they were responding to us?"

"They were responding to you," I tell him. "I didn't do much."

"Yeah, well, you're in the band. I can't do it without you."

"Of course you can."

"Well, I don't want to."

"Why not?"

He thinks about this while he's eating his pasta. He allows a little string of cheese to live on his lip for a second. I think about wiping it away. This is what women do for men all the time — prevent them from look-ing ridiculous. Finally he feels it and pulls it off, embarrassed, trying to hide it. As if men are smart enough to hide anything.

He takes a sip of wine and says, "You

really think I'm good enough?"

"I think you're too good," I tell him honestly.

"Too good for what?" he asks.

"I think you mean for who."

He raises an eyebrow. "You mean Jenny?"

"Is that her name? The redhead?"

"She's got a manager."

I push my plate away and lean over the table. I say, "Look, Franklin, you have talent, and everyone is in the business of stealing talent. You have to be able to recognize the thieves."

He hears this, then shakes his head. He's now overly involved with wiping his face off with his shredded paper napkin.

"Jenny's not like that," he tells me.

"Oh. And you know this because?"

"I'm instinctive about people," he informs me.

I laugh out loud. "The word is 'intuitive,' and only women are intuitive."

"You're just jealous," he tells me.

"Oh, really? What am I jealous of? Her hair? I know how to dye my hair red. I know how to wear a tank top. I know how to sing the way she sings. It's a trick. She's a trick. She's a siren, Franklin. She's leading you out onto the rocks. You can go there if you want to."

He squints his eyes at me. "And where are you leading me?"

"To the truth," I say.

"Your truth," he says, sitting up straighter in his chair.

"There is nothing relative about truth," I say.

"Okay, then," he counters. "Where's your manager?"

"I don't have one."

"Exactly."

"I'm just good at what I do."

"And Jenny isn't?"

"No, she's excellent at what she does. She steals talent."

Franklin looks at me for a long time. Confident that nothing unwanted is on his chin, he sits back in his chair and takes long, slow sips of his cheap red wine.

"You hate women, don't you?" he finally asks.

"I'm not sure. I don't think I know any."

"Why?"

"Because there aren't any women in Los Angeles. There are only little girls."

"What makes you say that?"

"Women have breasts and hips. Have you met anyone like that in L.A.?"

Smirking, he says, "I've met plenty of women with breasts."

"I mean real ones. You know how to tell the difference? Your breasts lie down when you do."

Franklin, who is smart, mulls this over, then says, "Do you know any men in Los Angeles?"

"There aren't many," I admit. "They're mostly girls in disguise."

"What am I, then?"

I think about that for a moment before I decide to answer honestly.

"You're a confused man."

"Oh, really?" he says, leaning away from me. "And what am I confused about?"

"Whether or not you are a man."

"And what's your definition of a man?"

I think about that for a moment. "Men fight," I say.

"Oh, you want me to join the army?"

"I don't want you to do anything. But that is my definition of men. They are willing to fight."

"What is it you want me to fight?" he asks.

"Jenny," I say.

We don't speak again until the check comes. When it does, we decide to divide it.

He's not a man, I realize to my dismay.

Men pay.

We are standing in front of the restaurant,

waiting for the parking valets to bring our car around, when I catch a glimpse of her. It's not a mistake. I'd know her anywhere. Our eyes connect, on this crowded street. She is in her late teens now. Either she's pursuing her path to greatness or she has given up. Her clothes tell me she's chosen the latter. She's dirty and distracted. She's not carrying a violin.

Franklin is yammering about how he could have played the last solo better. It was good, but it could have been better. I feel trapped by his narcissism, and I'm not listening anymore because I have seen her and I want to follow her. She is walking away from me, walking alone, moving rather blindly down the empty sidewalk.

I say, "Hallie!"

The body freezes, then, without looking back, starts to move faster.

"Hallie, is that you?" I call out.

She walks even faster.

Then I abandon Franklin and start to run down the sidewalk. I am gaining on her when she spins around and looks at me. It's her and it isn't her. Her hair is red now. Her skin is the same amount of pale. Her eyes connect with mine, and they say, Don't come any closer.

"It's me," I say. "Your music teacher."

This person, who looks so much like Hallie but might not be, says, "I don't have a music teacher."

Our eyes connect.

She says, "Look, just leave me alone."

I move closer to her. It's as if she's a ghost and I'm afraid she'll go back to some other dimension.

I say, "Hallie, I know I screwed everything up. I didn't want to hurt you. I just wanted to save you."

"Save me?" Her expression is one of genuine bewilderment. "Who are you, thinking you can save people?"

I have no answer to that. "Just stay. Stay and talk to me."

"You are scary," she says to me.

"No, I'm really not."

Then she disappears around the corner.

I watch her walk away, and I'm not sure. I thought it was her — I would have bet my life on it — but as I see her disappearing into the shadows, she seems like some flimsy bet I put on myself. I don't know anymore. I don't know anything.

She moves into darkness, and I stand there. Finally I move back to where Franklin is waiting.

He says, "What was that all about?"

"I thought I knew her."

He rolls his eyes, then looks up to heaven, as if he's seen the light.

He says, "Jesus, Pearl, if you're gay, just say so."

"I'm not gay. I thought I knew her."

He just looks at me.

"I thought it was Hallie," I tell him.

He sighs. "Your student? That Hallie?"

"Yes."

"That was months ago. Aren't you over that?"

No, I am not over that. I will never be over that.

But I don't trust him enough to say it.

"Tell me what went on there. A student left you? Is that the big deal?"

"No, it was more."

"What?"

I can't look at him.

His car arrives, he tips the valet, and as he's climbing in, he calls out to me, "I think this is the beginning of a beautiful friendship."

"Maybe," I respond, watching him get in the car and drive off.

I don't say, First you have to believe in those things.

It wasn't just that she was good. I won't bore you with the details of how good she was. Musicians can be so tedious about details. And the truth is, it's never about details or technicalities. It's always about feel. When a musician is truly gifted, it is because she has tapped into something entirely beyond definition. She hears the music. She captures it. She processes her own emotions through it. She explains it, without defining it. Sometimes I wish God would give me the words to describe it; other times, I'm grateful that he doesn't. She was good, all right? She was blessed.

And sometimes I think that what happened to her had everything to do with my own pride, my own expectations. I had already started to brag about her. I couldn't resist telling Franklin and Ernest (the two most arrogant musicians) that I had struck gold with this student, that I had found the person who would put all of us on the map. I pictured us going to see her at the philharmonic, taking up an entire reserved row. I pictured her announcing to the audience that we were there, giving us credit for her accomplishment. Truth be told, I pictured her singling me out and asking me to take a bow.

But that was just an indulgence on my part. Mainly I focused on teaching her, drawing those sounds from her, luxuriating in the perfection of her playing.

So you can imagine how I felt when, seven or eight months in, she told me she was quitting.

I told her she couldn't.

She said, "We're out of money. We can't pay anymore."

"What about the state grant?"

"It ran out."

"I don't believe you," I told her. "Dorothy hasn't said anything."

"Earl knows," she said. "He told me last night. The money has stopped coming in."

I sighed, resting in my metal chair, taking a moment to stare at her and devise a plan. I didn't know Earl at all, but I pictured him as this big, mean, opposing man who commanded the obedience of all the women in his life. I saw Dorothy cowering in his presence, letting the gleam in her eye leak out and drift down the drain. They had boys who were into sports. Earl was probably the commander. He understood men competing with one another and nothing else. He was eager to give up on her.

"Then you have to find the money somewhere else," I told her.

"Where?" she asked.

"There are all kinds of ways. You can't just give up. You're truly gifted."

She shrugged, putting her instrument away long before we were finished.

"He doesn't want me playing anymore," she told me.

Earl. The cold-eyed commander.

I sat forward in my seat and reached out for her hand. She allowed me to take it. There were no marks on her wrist. It was as if I had dreamed it. Now I was only trying to reach my best student, trying to persuade her to realize my dreams along with hers.

I knew, even as I did it, that this was a shortcoming of my profession. Wanting to achieve through your students is the strongest drug any teacher can ever confront. I wanted to be above that, but I wasn't.

I said, "Hallie, listen to me. I know you've had a hard life, but music is the way out. You can't just abandon it. It's showing you how to live."

She looked down at her scuffed Doc Martens. "I don't care about how to live."

I squeezed her hand, but her expression did not change. She stared at the ground as if she expected nothing from it, which was why she longed for it.

"You don't know how hard it is," she finally said.

"I think I know a little about it," I told her. And then I told her the whole story of my own abandoned violin, melting among the leaves, and how I finally made it to college and found the music again. I had always thought my story was pretty impressive, but Hallie did not seem swayed by it. Eventually she looked up at me.

"There comes a point," she said, "where it's no longer worth it."

There was something mature in her tone of voice, but I chose to ignore it.

Still stuck in teacher mode, I said, "Don't you dare say that. Music is always worth it. It's worth everything and anything. I'll talk to Dorothy. I'll make it work."

She shook her head vigorously. "No, don't do that."

"You don't understand," I said, allowing some of my own desperation to creep through. "When you are good, when you have real talent, you also have a moral obligation to develop it, to see where it intends to take you."

She lifted her eyes to me, at the same time withdrawing her hand from mine. She chewed on a hangnail, her eyes trained on my face.

"I have a moral obligation?" she asked.

"Yes."

"Like God? He's going to punish me if I stop?"

Had I not been so desperate in that moment, I would have told the truth. I would have said, Oh, Hallie, who the hell knows about God or his intentions? I only know that I would do almost anything to possess your talent, so I'm willing to do almost anything to make sure that, at least in you, it is realized. That is a teacher's obligation, is it not? A teacher shows her student how to do what she herself is not capable of, not courageous enough to pursue.

Instead, because I was on a roll, I said, "It's not the kind of punishment you're thinking of. If you give up, your punishment will be to walk around in this world, a true musician without an instrument. A player without a place to play."

She stared at the ground, maybe at her feet, maybe at something I could not see.

"You don't want to give up, do you?" I asked.

She shrugged. "It's part of my father, part of my mother. It's the only thing I love."

"Well, there you go," I said, feeling a tenuous victory.

She sighed a long sigh and lifted the instrument to her chin. She raised the bow shoulder-high and looked at me again.

"So anything is worth it?" she asked.

"Anything," I told her.

147

As if I knew. As if I had a fucking clue.

The money, somehow, did not give out. She kept coming in for lessons. Dorothy kept writing checks. The world kept turning; it didn't end. And Hallie kept making beautiful sounds.

I held on to my dreams, and to hers, locking them both away in a safe place. A place of isolation, devoid of conscience, devoid of regret. I pondered it in my heart.

All criminals have a deep need to confess.

My father, the carpenter, confessed to me by taking me to see fires being put out.

He loved fire the way I love music, and he could not keep it to himself. He told me how fires started. He told me how they were extinguished.

All criminals confess to their crimes through their obsessions. Sex addicts pretend to be celibate. Thieves pretend to admire cops. Arsonists pretend to worship firefighters.

There was a tradition in my house, in my lonely house in Virginia, with my two angry parents, who mostly hated life and refused to participate in it until the fire alarm went off. Then my father would wake me up, regardless of the hour, and load me into the car, and we would chase the fire.

My father loved wood, and he equally and curiously loved the thing that could destroy it.

It was up to him which entity he preferred over the other. Creation or destruction is always the choice. He worried over both. I sat still and waited to learn.

I think, in some part of my brain, that I committed to birth rather than death. Which didn't make me weak. It just made me, as I see it, a woman.

Much later, when he saw me falling in love with an instrument, he wanted to say, Yes, I've known a love like that, quite apart from what you feel for another person. The love you feel for a force, for the evidence of God on earth. He loved fire, but he had no real place to worship it. He loved fire too much to kill it. Much as I ultimately loved music too much to kill it.

We are, of course, destroyed by what we love.

9

Who was the greatest lyricist who ever lived?

Patrick says, "Paul Simon."

Ernest says, "Steve Earle."

Clive says, "Bruce Springsteen. No, John Lennon. No, Elvis Costello. No, Bruce."

I say, "Woody Guthrie."

Franklin says, "Who the hell cares about lyrics?"

It is a Wednesday night. We are closing up shop, and we're all somewhat behind, since the holidays are closing in and the store has been very busy. I am cranky, mainly because it is December and I have no one to celebrate with, but also because, generally speaking, I need to get laid, and not getting laid really does make a woman cranky. Music almost does the trick, but eventually it doesn't. Eventually the keeper of the music realizes that it isn't quite the same as sex, and then the keeper of the music gets a little agitated, knowing that sex would actually help her sleep. But she doesn't know where to get it. No, that's not entirely true. She could get it from the twenty-eight-year-old bass player, but she doesn't want to do that. She wants to get it from the store manager, the only real man in evidence, but he's so obsessed with music, which he thinks is better than getting laid, that he can't imagine the real thing anymore.

The bottom line is this: life is about people interacting with one another. When people resist doing that, they go a little crazy. They start demanding more than can reasonably be expected from things like musical instruments or pets or houseplants or hobbies. Or students.

The fact that none of us, the lost souls at McCoy's, have any real receptacle for our physical passions explains why we hang around talking about who was the greatest lyricist. It's fine to talk about those things. It's really not fine to pretend that it matters in any kind of picture, let alone the big one.

It is because of this essential spiritual deficiency that I became overly involved with Hallie. It is fair to say that her talent attracted me. It is fair to say that I wanted her to realize her potential and that I, as her teacher, felt obligated to do my best to make that happen. It is fine and admirable to want to do your job well. When you want your job to define you, fill up all your holes, make up for what is missing, justify your existence, and serve as a stand-in for your own lost ambitions . . . well, this is when you get into trouble.

That is what happened when I made the decision to visit Hallie's home.

About a month after I saw the bruising on her wrists, a few weeks after she'd told me the money had run out, I noticed that she showed up at our lessons looking depressed and withdrawn. She practiced her scales without complaining. From a technical standpoint, she played all her exercises with perfect precision. But her heart was not in it. The music itself, which is connected to something much deeper than finger and wrist movements, had gone away. It was dying, if not dead. When you see that happen, you know that the student has reached the end of her journey. In most cases, you simply let the lack of interest run its course. The student starts showing up late, starts complaining, stops practicing, stops caring. I had always accepted that with my students. Maybe I would have a couple of concerned discussions with the frustrated parents, but I didn't have much to offer once the interest started bleeding out of the student. It was an exercise, telling everyone to stay the course. I really knew that the course was over, and I simply waited for it to become apparent to all concerned.

I refused to do that with Hallie. When I saw her going through the motions, I decided to do a thing that I never did. I called Dorothy and asked if I could come out for a visit. She didn't resist me. She was eager for it. It was clear to me that Hallie's proficiency in violin was the only thing that kept her interested in this sullen child.

The home was in a pleasant little pocket of Mar Vista, which literally means "view of the sea." The sea was close enough to be a rumor in that part of town, but the community was tucked away behind the airport, closer to large warehouse stores and fast-food chains and enormous prefabricated apartment buildings. The ugliness of the landscape had earned this part of town the nickname Marred Vista. I kind of respected that.

It was an ordinary weekday evening when I showed up at their house in my exhausted Honda. My backseat was full of sheet music and accoutrements for my violin, but I left the car unlocked, knowing that no one is in the business of stealing actual music. They only steal radios and CDs. They steal technology. I learned this when my car was broken into in front of my house. I had gotten lazy and left my violin in the backseat. The thieves left it and took, instead, forty dollars' worth of CDs. I suppose it's the good news that no one knows where music really comes from or how much it is really worth.

Dorothy let me into the house, which was small but clean and well kept in the way that poor people's houses are. Everything was cheap, but it gleamed. Just like the house I grew up in. I can remember my mother saying, "We don't have much, but you can eat off it." She thought that only rich people had the luxury of being dirty. She might have remembered that from when her family had money. The Millners' house had been messier than ours, but the mess seemed grand somehow. Book scattered, clothes left on the floor, jewelry tossed on countertops. As if there were more where that came from. In a certain kind of poor people's house, everything always matches. Those are the poor people with aspirations. Trying to step up and blend in with the class hovering just above them. Matching sets of furniture, and rugs that match the upholstery, and gewgaws and color schemes that tie everything together.

As if symmetry begets beauty.

The Edwardses' house greeted me with all that and a thousand smells. Carpet was everywhere, and it held the landscape of their existence. Pledge and smoke and air fresheners, food and pets and perfume. Dorothy yelled for her husband as she offered me a seat, and Earl appeared as if he'd been waiting offstage for his cue.

He was a tall man, well built, but with a cowering nature. He looked at me with watery blue eyes. He still had on his suit from work, even the jacket, and he was completely devoid of wrinkles. He sat on the edge of his La-Z-Boy recliner and interlaced his long fingers and waited.

"I am Pearl Swain, Hallie's music teacher —"

He clipped my sentence. "Is the girl giving you trouble?"

"No, not at all," I said.

"Can I get you some coffee?" Dorothy asked. "My boys are at sports practice. One plays basketball. The other one wrestles. It's never-ending around here."

"No, I don't need coffee. Where is Hallie?"

"In her room," Earl answered. "Doing her homework. I'm not usually home this early. Dorothy told me you were coming. What's the problem?"

"Earl is in insurance," Dorothy interjected.

Earl cast a glance at her.

"There's no problem," I said.

"I don't understand," he said.

I began to feel a queasiness building in my stomach, like the early stages of the flu or pregnancy, when it's possible to tell yourself it's not there. The tightness grew with my resistance to it. I couldn't tell where it was coming from — the smells from the carpet or the familiar surroundings or the unnatural stillness of Earl.

He squinted at me, and I said, "Well, there's a slight problem, in that Hallie is exceptionally talented but lately I see her losing heart."

"Is she talking back?"

"No, nothing like that."

"Because I don't tolerate back talk."

"We have discussions. I'm interested in her opinion."

"Because I tell her like I tell my boys. You can't help how smart or good looking you are, but you can sure help how you behave."

The queasiness leapt forward. My father might have said something just like that to me. I wondered if I looked as pale as I felt.

"So what is it, then?" he asked.

Dorothy seemed to check out, her loquacious nature disappearing in the presence of her husband. I saw how he ruled this house with his exactitude. His quiet dominion. His inscrutable expression. I had seen my father do that when company came. When the preacher dropped by. When my mother threw a fit. He was proving to us that he would not be moved even as everything moved around him.

I said, "It's nothing I can put a finger on. It's more like a feeling. Hallie showed some real aptitude in music, with the violin in particular. Which is a hard instrument to play. But now she just seems to be going through the motions."

Earl smiled at me. He had a large head. His hair was thick and carefully combed back. "Going through the motions, is that what you said?"

"Yes."

"Isn't that what she's supposed to do? Isn't that what a teacher asks a student to do?"

"Technically speaking. What I mean is, she doesn't care."

"If she doesn't care, she should stop."

"She used to care, though."

I couldn't believe the way my brain was breaking down. Something in his manner was scrambling my thoughts. His expression was neutral, but I could feel the sneer building inside him. I knew I could not say the words. They were as scorned here as in my father's house.

"She used to care and now she doesn't," he repeated.

"Going through the motions works in certain things, but not in music. You have to have a kind of . . . interest in it."

He knew I meant "passion." He knew all the words I was talking around.

He smiled. "Well, I don't have my heart set on her being a musician. Do you, Dorothy?"

Dorothy's eyes grazed mine. Then she said, "It would be nice if she had a marketable skill."

"Typing. That's a marketable skill."

"Well, yes, but I don't see why she couldn't do both."

"Miss . . . Swain, is it? I know you have to get all wrapped up in your students because they pay you and whatnot. But Hallie came to us carrying that violin and talking about playing it. Now, if she's changed her mind, I'm going to have to let that be."

"I happen to know, Mr. Edwards, that Hallie only came to me because someone in school recognized her talent and suggested she apply for a grant. At which point Mrs. Edwards brought her in. Hallie herself was reluctant to take the lessons. After a few lessons, she began to come into her own. She showed a kind of talent that I have never seen in my years of teaching. And soon her devotion to the music developed. I saw it happen right before my eyes. I saw her grow into it. I didn't imagine it."

"No one's saying you did," he said evenly.

"And then I saw it disappear. Now, as a teacher, I am supposed to pay attention to my student's behavior. I have an obligation to let the parents know when I see some kind of abrupt change like that. Sometimes it's indicative of something —"

I cut myself off. They were staring at me. Dorothy sucked in a breath and put a manicured hand to her mouth.

"Drugs?" she asked. Hopefully, I thought.

I stared hard at her. "No. Not drugs."

"Something worse?" she asked.

I looked at Earl. His expression had not changed.

He said, "I don't think you're that kind of teacher. You're not a public school teacher. Those are the people who are supposed to let us know when something's wrong. Her math teacher. Her history teacher. Those folks. Not you. She pays to see you. Or should I say, we pay for her to see you."

"Yes, it's true. I'm not actually a mandated

reporter. But I am concerned. And I can't ignore that concern."

"What's a mandated reporter?" Dorothy asked.

Earl ignored her. "That she's losing interest in music. That's your concern."

I leaned toward him. "That she's experiencing some kind of extreme stress."

A door opened abruptly, and Hallie came in, wearing a hoodie and pajama bottoms, her hair wet and combed back. She looked like an innocent girl. Not the dark, sullen creature who always stomped up the stairs.

"I can't study," she said. "It's too loud."

Dorothy cast her eyes to the far wall.

Hallie froze when she saw me.

"What are you doing here?"

"Just checking in. I told you I might."

"No, you didn't."

"I wanted to update your parents . . . Mr. and Mrs. Edwards . . . on your progress."

"Bullshit."

"Hey, young lady," Earl said.

"She's lying. She's telling you that I did something wrong."

"Did you do something wrong?" he asked.

"No. But teachers don't ever come around with good news."

I said, "Hallie, this is really between the three of us, so if you could just go back to your room. We'll keep our voices down. It's nothing important."

She gave me a hard look. "Whatever she's telling you is something she's made up in her own mind."

She slammed the door, and we listened to her familiar stomp going away.

The Edwardses were looking at me.

"Well, look, I'm not objective. I just want Hallie to continue on this path," I said.

"You let us worry about her path," Earl said.

Dorothy was looking away from him.

"Thanks for stopping by," he said.

He walked me to the door. Dorothy didn't move.

When we got there, he put a hand on my shoulder, and the tightness moved through my stomach again.

"Do you have children, Miss Swain?"

"No. Just my students."

"There aren't many people like you left in the world."

I laughed. "You mean crazy musicians? There are. Way too many."

"I meant people who care," he said. The sudden shift in his tone confused me until I realized that because I was leaving, he no longer saw me as a threat. His defenses were down, and his true nature was emerging.

He had been scared. That was where the demeanor came from. The unwillingness to reveal anything of himself.

Sometimes I forgot how much men had to hide.

"I do appreciate your interest in my daughter."

Dorothy spoke up then, moving in our direction. The attention had been off her for long enough.

"We get the point, Earl."

Earl said to me, "What's your first name, again?"

"Pearl."

"Earl with a *P*."

He laughed at his own joke.

This was the final straw for Dorothy. She was standing right next to her husband now, her dark eyes bearing down on me.

"Good night, Miss Swain."

I didn't know what was going on in this house. But whatever it was, a deal had been struck. There was a common agreement. Something so solid and oppressive that even Hallie was unwilling to betray it. There was no question of that. The only question left was how much of it was my business.

Franklin ducks out early this Wednesday night, shortly after our best-lyricist discus-

162

sion. He has a gig with his new friend Jenny. He tells me he's not really in her band, he's just sitting in tonight, playing for an adult birthday party in Bel Air, at the home of a movie director. He assures me that this is good for the Trailer Park Rogues, as he can make some connections. I say, "Yeah, I know all about the connections you're trying to make." The memory of Jenny is clear in my mind. She is young and still looks good in a tank top. Her vocal style is a trick. It's vibrato taken to an unholy level. It's a warble. It's a step away from yodeling. But Franklin is falling for it. And maybe I'm the fool for not realizing that I was being set up.

Franklin just shakes his head at me and says, "Pearl, you know, a musical marriage is even harder than the real kind."

I say, "What would you know about either one?"

But he only chuckles and goes out. Ernest follows him, with his own battered Gibson in a beat-up case, saying he's going to try to hook up with this married woman he's pursuing, whose husband is a shithead lawyer who works all the time, leaving her lonely and vulnerable. "Is she pretty?" I ask him. "For a woman her age, she's a fox," he says proudly, as if he's figured something out. Older women have some hidden value, and he alone has discovered it, like a guy who has discovered a new planet. I don't ask how old she is. I'm sure that she's several years younger than I am and that it never occurred to Ernest that I might be offended. Because it never occurred to Ernest that I'm capable of having an affair.

I say to his back, "It's his money that's keeping her attractive. Pilates! Botox! It's expensive to look young when you're old!"

But the door slams halfway through my retort.

I wonder if I'm capable of having an affair.

And then I am left alone with Patrick, who is leaning against the far wall, without an instrument, smiling at me.

"What?" I say.

He shakes his head. His long hair is pulled back into a ponytail.

"Who is it you're really talking to?" he asks.

"Oh, leave me alone," I say, grabbing my violin. "Paul Simon is a fraud. He writes poems and then he hires other cultures to arrange the music, but he takes all the credit."

Patrick shrugs. "But he writes the poems."

"That's not hard. It's only half the equation."

Patrick shrugs again.

"So write me one," he says.

"What?"

"Write me a poem if they're so easy."

Actually, he says "sho easy."

I glare at him.

I say, "You're not walking me to my car."

He shrugs again. "Why would I do that?"

"Because all the men in this place volunteer to do that when they want something."

"I don't want anything from you," he says.

"Good," I say.

I make it all the way to the door with my violin bumping against my rib cage. Then I hear him say, "I just want you to know who I am."

I turn on him, already agitated. "Oh, really? Who are you?"

He shrugs again.

I say, "You want me to know who you are? Tell me what instrument you play."

The smile dissolves from his face, even though no other muscle in his body moves.

"I told you before," he says.

"Tell me again."

He looks hard at me. His eyes are the color of rain, and the definition of piercing. His face is all angles. His chin juts out toward me. He is tall and thin and lean, but he is not young.

"I play all of them," he says.

"You play all instruments?"

My hands are shaking and the rest of my body will soon follow. I can't stand being this close to him, though there is an entire store and several musical instruments separating us.

I feel as though we are neck and neck.

Photo finish. But with no finish.

"Okay, fine," I say, knowing that there are such people in the world who literally play all instruments. They are few and far between. They have perfect pitch. They can pick up anything devised to make music and elicit beautiful sounds. They don't fight with their instruments or worry about them or stand in awe of them. They create partnerships first, and then they master them. For them, the mystery is more than half solved, and maybe it's why they put the instrument down. Maybe it accounts for their lack of concern. Maybe it's why Patrick has nothing to worry about.

"What was your first instrument?" I ask him. "What did you learn on?"

He barely moves. He says, "I didn't learn on any of them."

"What? You were born knowing?"

He nods.

"I was born knowing," he says.

"You're full of shit," I tell him.

He laughs. "Well, sure. I'm full of shit. I'm human."

"You can't even remember the first time —"

"My first instrument was probably this," he says. He puts the ends of his fingers into his ears. Takes them out. Puts them in again.

I stare at him.

"The roar," he explains. "When you plug your ears. What is the roar? The sound of your blood? The engine of your brain? This is what led me to music. Instruments are everywhere. Why do you people worry yourselves with details?"

"That's just noise."

"I think it's in the ear of the beholder — what is noise and what isn't."

"I think that's a cop-out."

Patrick smiles. "Now you're talking like Franklin. You only like him because he doesn't approve of you. And if he doesn't approve, you can never get close."

"That's just not true."

"Truth. Another subjective discussion."

"Good night, Patrick."

He says something, but it is lost in the sound of the door closing behind me, obscured by the ringing of some strange chime Franklin put there long ago to warn us that someone had arrived, in search of music.

10

You might be wondering how a woman gets to be forty in a city as big as Los Angeles without having any female friends. Well, I did have them. Or I had one. Her name was Leah.

We used to meet at John O'Groats, an Irish breakfast joint on Pico, every other Saturday morning to catch up. Leah was a lawyer-turned-artist. She worked in family law. She dropped out and took up mixed media, which, as far as I could tell, was about putting unlikely stuff together until it looked good. She said that's what families were about, too. But with art, nobody gets hurt.

Leah made a name for herself by collecting bottle caps, flattening them with an iron, painting them, and then arranging them into abstract forms on a piece of plywood. There was a real rush for her work a few years back. Celebrities bought it. (That's how you know you've made it in L.A.) Leah would call me at all hours, saying, "Oh, my God, Tom Cruise was just here!" Or George Clooney or Jennifer Lopez or Susan Sarandon. Like most art waves in Los Angeles, it didn't last long.

We met at church, when I first moved here. A laid-back Episcopal church, which never bothered with follow-up. My faith started dwindling around the breakup of my marriage, and the church was so laid back they never sent anyone to check on me. This just didn't seem right to me. Though at the time, Leah said, "Pearl, be honest. If they sent someone, you'd throw a bucket of piss in their face."

I would never have done that, but it sounded appealing.

I said, "Well, I'd like the option."

Leah laughed her raspy smoker's laugh and said, "That's why preachers stopped making house calls. Who wants to get pissed on without a soul to show for it?"

Leah still went to church, even though she had been flailing as an artist. Or maybe because of it. She liked her faith. Whenever we talked, she'd say, "Don't you miss the wafer, Pearl? Don't you want to take Communion?"

"What for?"

"For protection," she said.

"Protection against what?"

"Well, I don't know. Life."

"I don't think it works that way. That's more like superstition."

"It's not a superstition. It's an image. An archetype. Jesus is your lawyer. Communion is your retainer."

"Please." I kind of believed it. But at the same time, as a musician, I thought I was way more up in God's grill than Leah. Although flattening out bottle caps might have had a spiritual component, I hadn't yet understood. I have always believed in art, have devoted myself to it from an early age, because I decided it was important to make the world a more beautiful place. But the bottle caps sometimes looked to me like a nervous preoccupation, an attempt to ward something off. It scared me when I thought that music might have become that for me, too.

Leah and I had our bimonthly breakfast at John O'Groats shortly after my visit to the Edwardses'. I usually filled her in on all the happenings at my job. It took the place of her isolated life, experimenting in art while she whittled away at the same married man she'd been seeing for years. His name was Phillip. He was a literary agent.

He was never going to leave his wife.

Leah was beautiful and still made every effort to keep herself that way. She wore whites and creams to show off her black hair and olive skin. She wore all kinds of rattling jewelry and she always smelled like something exotic. People stared at her.

Next to her, I felt dowdy but somehow proud of my earth tones and bare arms. As if I were a more serious person.

Leah always asked about my love life. Even back then, I made the mistake of telling her about Clive.

She was excited. She said, "Why shouldn't you sleep with a young guy? What's the harm in it?"

"He's young. And we work together."

"If you sleep with him, the other guy will come around in no time."

"You mean Franklin? I'm not sure I want him, either."

"Well, who do you want?"

"I don't know."

"Pearl, you haven't had sex in ages. Have you? You're all alone in that crappy place and you're waiting for Mark to leave Stephanie."

"No, I'm not." But back then, I might have been.

"You need to start living."

"You're hanging around every night, waiting for a married man to call you."

"And how are we so different?"

"I'm not desperate."

"You're not?"

"Okay. I'm aware of my desperation. But you're in retreat."

"Not forever."

"Oh, really? How can you be sure?"

"Because I don't have a vibrator."

"How is this proof of anything?"

"When you get one, you're giving up."

"That's not true."

We had that argument often. I was right, though. I knew a lot of girls who had stopped looking after crossing that Rubicon.

"Is it really so much better," I asked her, "to sleep with a man who is emotionally connected to someone else?"

"He's only legally connected to her."

"Right. What planet are you on?"

"He's staying for the children."

"The children are in college."

This seemed to hurt her a little, but she was far too tough to admit it.

She sighed and said, "Oh, Pearl, I don't know. You're going home alone tonight, and so am I, but I have the chance of someone calling me in the morning. And he'll come over in the evening and we'll make love. And I won't be alone for those hours. Do you have anything like it?"

I didn't have anything like that. But I could pick up an instrument and play it and I wouldn't have to tell it anything in the morning.

Still, I missed lying next to someone in a bed. Kicking him when he got too close or snored. Forgetting he was there, then remembering. Looking dumbfounded at each other when the morning broke through the blind. Wondering who was going to shiver and say, "It's cold." Wondering who was going to make the coffee. Wondering who was going to say, "Coffee can wait."

I remember thinking all this. I remember the whole conversation because I could have left it there. I didn't have to say the thing I said next. I didn't have to set it all in motion.

I said, "Listen, I need some advice. I have a situation at work."

She laughed. "I told you. Sleep with the bass player."

"It's about this student I'm working with. She's kind of a foster kid. She's not in the system, but she's living with some relatives who inherited her."

"Uh-huh," she said. She didn't look up.

She said this in a tone that asked me not to go further. She used to deal in custody cases, representing parents warring over their children, and sometimes representing the children who had been taken out of dysfunctional homes in order to be placed in less (though not always) dysfunctional situations. She understood about abuse and Social Services and when a layperson was required to step in. She understood, but she left it all behind to flatten bottle caps. She had told me before that it was the pain that turned her away. And I could see the pain rising to the surface again, like some recurring nightmare she couldn't fight off. As if it always hovered. I felt bad for bringing it up, but I had to.

I said, "Suppose I suspect some kind of abuse is going on."

"What kind?"

"I saw bruises. On her wrists. She said she was wrestling with her brothers. Her cousins. The boys she's living with."

"Right."

"But I think there's more."

"What do you think it is?"

"I don't know. I just have a feeling that something very bad is happening."

"Feelings don't play out in court, Pearl."

"I went to the house. I met her foster

father. He gave me a stomachache."

"How did he do that?"

I pushed my plate away and leaned forward. "I know about unhappy homes, Leah. I know them when I'm around them."

"Leave it alone," she said quietly.

"There's something going on. I can't say what, but I know it. She has suddenly lost interest in the music. She's really talented and she used to love it. Now she just phones it in. Isn't that indicative of something really bad?"

"Not necessarily. It could be indicative of anything. Hormones. Anything."

"So you're telling me to stand by and do nothing?"

"I haven't heard anything concrete. Believe me, Pearl, it's hard enough to prove these cases when you have hard evidence. I can't tell you the times I went to court with signed depositions from abused kids, only to have them recant on the stand. And even when I got some of these kids out of their homes, I just threw them into the frying pan. We all fall in love with the fairy-tale ending. The beauty of riding in and rescuing these children and delivering them to some better place. Sometimes there isn't a better place. And I came to the conclusion that maybe the stories we are born with are nothing more than that. Just our stories. Everybody has something to get through. Everybody has something to live down."

"I think that's harsh."

"You don't know harsh. You only imagine it. I've seen it. Trust me, you don't want to go there. Just teach them and send them home. Clock out, for God's sake."

"What kind of world is it when people just stop looking out for each other?"

"I don't know what kind of world it is. I just know it's the one we live in."

We were silent for a moment. We sipped our coffee and she avoided my eyes.

Finally she looked up. "Maybe this is about your own childhood and you need to go to therapy."

"It's not about my childhood. Though I don't deny I'm sensitive to her plight. It's how I'm able to recognize it."

"Then maybe it's about you having nothing else in your life."

"Oh. I see. So if I get a vibrator, I can learn to ignore pain?"

"If not ignore it, at least keep it at bay."

"Until what? I'm strong enough to confront it?"

"No. Until you're strong enough to realize that it is always going to exist. And these distractions — music, art, sex, movie pop-corn, alcohol, whatever you choose — serve as a vacation from it all. Not an escape. Just a stepping out."

I looked down and pinched my lips against the angry things I wanted to say.

"That's what church is, Pearl. If you went back you'd understand. It's just a stepping out of the world. For that one hour. If that's all you can afford, it's enough. But if you can't step out at all, the world gets to be too much."

"I barely live in it at all. Isn't that your argument? I'm not at the party?"

"You're in it," she said. "But you're only in it for the bad parts. Even your music makes you sad."

"No, it doesn't."

"Yes, it does. It reminds you of some lost career. It reminds you of Mark. It reminds you of your father. It never puts you in the moment or makes you look ahead."

"You don't know the first thing about my music."

"I know what you've told me."

I didn't feel like talking anymore. I felt defeated but not wrong. I felt overwhelmed by what she was saying to me. She didn't know my life at all, and I didn't know hers. She had walked from pain into art and had found some kind of relief. I had walked from pain into art and found more pain. This, she was saying, was how we differed. She was telling me to feel less. She was telling me to look away. But when we look away, there's no art. There is only distraction.

She said, "Look, if you are really concerned, I know someone in Social Services you can talk to. But it's a slippery slope, and you'd better think very hard about it before you get involved."

I didn't respond. We gathered our things and left.

We said good-bye on the street with a wooden hug. She went off to her car and I went off to buy some vacuum cleaner bags.

If I'm honest, that was the moment I shut down the possibility of Clive. Even though Leah had said it was okay. Even though Leah was who I went to for permission. Because I thought she really knew how to live.

I stood in the vacuum cleaner store, looking at the bags, of which there were too many kinds, and I was unable to remember the model number of my vacuum cleaner, because I didn't give a shit, and an Armenian man with anxious eyes was heading in my direction, and I realized, I don't love Leah anymore, and if I don't love Leah anymore, I'm not sure who I love, and if I don't love anyone, that means no one loves me, and people cannot live without love. They've done studies.

By the time the Armenian man reached me, I had started to cry, and he said, "What can I do for you?"

And I looked at him and said, "Nothing."

That Monday was when I got the news.

It was at the end of a lesson, during which Hallie had done a fine job of memorizing the first movement of a Bach concerto, that she told me. She was memorizing now, had been for some time, which meant she was no longer reading music. She was storing it all in her brain, and it came out by the numbers, technically perfect, spiritually bland. The thrill was gone, for both of us, and occasionally we looked at each other like old friends who could no longer remember our shared past, all the reasons we liked each other. Like me and Leah.

"Very nice," I said.

She put her violin on her lap and sighed.

"What's up with you?" I asked, hoping that innocent question would help us segue into something more meaningful. I was hoping to dig deep into her psyche, help her root out the reasons she no longer cared about her music. As it turned out, her problems were gestating at the surface of her brain, waiting to hatch on her tongue.

She looked at me, her dark eyes flat and devoid of emotion, her eyebrow ring dull and placid in the harsh fluorescent light.

She said, "I think I'm pregnant."

Nothing could have prepared me for that. I heard it, dismissed it, heard it again, and started thinking. My face must have processed a dozen emotions at once, and she looked away from me, down at her scuffed Doc Martens.

"How?" I said, without thinking.

She looked up at me, surprised for a second, before she smirked.

"Are you sure?" I asked.

"No. What does it feel like?"

I didn't know how to tell her. I had been pregnant, twice, had lost both babies. The first time I barely knew I was pregnant. The second time I knew right away, having grown accustomed to the symptoms. It was an indescribable feeling. In the early days, it felt like being plugged up, with a thick, warm water collecting at the drain. It made you feel drowsy and cranky and warm and cold. It made your breasts come alive, though they weren't sure what to do with their new life. I had headaches and backaches and a vague flulike sensation. But those could have been the symptoms of anything.

"You're not pregnant," I told her. Then all the ramifications of that statement went through my head, as quickly as information through a computer circuit, and I said, "Hallie, you're only fourteen."

"I know," she said.

"Why are you fooling around?" I asked.

She shrugged, chewing on a hangnail.

"If you are fooling around, why aren't you using birth control?"

She shrugged again. Then she said, "Tell me what to do."

"Get rid of it," I said without hesitation. Because here was this fourteen-year-old girl on the verge of greatness, musically speaking, and I couldn't imagine letting her take this event another step further. I couldn't imagine it was God's will to let a fourteen-year-old musical prodigy end it all by having a baby.

She had no reaction to my advice. She continued to stare at the floor.

"Does Dorothy know?" I asked.

"No," she said quickly. "And you can't tell her. You're like a shrink or a priest or something. It's against the law for you to tell anyone."

I had to admit, I liked being put in the category of a shrink or a priest, but the truth was, I was only a teacher, not a public school teacher, as Earl had pointed out, and I had no obligation to anyone. I could tell the cops, the social workers, the parents, anyone. The only thing forcing me to keep this secret was the thin specter of loyalty.

"Do you need money?" I asked.

She shook her head.

"You do if you want an abortion," I told her.

She glanced up at me. "How much are they?"

"I don't know. At least five hundred for a good one."

She picked at a hangnail and said, "I don't have that kind of cash."

I grew angry all of a sudden, picturing the seventeen-year-old piece of trash who had done this to her, some swaggering senior who told her it wouldn't hurt and it wouldn't count if they were standing up, and she'd never get pregnant because it doesn't happen the first time.

And that was the positive scenario I was picturing. The other one wouldn't quite form.

"What's he, a football player?" I asked.

She shook her head, still staring at the ground.

"Basketball? Some kind of jock? Some kind of Best All-Around?"

"No."

"Another musician? Some kid in a band?"

"No."

"How did he talk you into it?"

She shrugged. "He didn't do much talking."

"It's illegal, you know," I told her. "You're underage. It's statutory rape."

"Oh, what, are you going to tell the cops?"

"It's certainly an option," I said.

"Not to me. And if you tell anybody, you're going to make me very sorry I said anything. I'll deny it."

I cleared my throat and tried to gather my thoughts.

"Does he know?" I asked.

She laughed a short, derisive laugh. "We don't talk about things like that."

"Well, that's exactly what you should be talking about. You should have talked about it before."

"I know. That's what they say in health class, but that's not how it is."

"He has certain obligations," I said.

She shrugged again. She looked very tired. She started putting her violin and her music sheets into her case. She was giving up. On both of us.

I said, "If I give you the money, do you promise to get it taken care of?"

Her eyes came alive. She looked like a kid being offered a day at the fair.

"Yes, I promise."

"I can get the money for you. We can work this out. But Hallie, you have to tell me if this is something else. I mean, something besides some high school boy."

"I never said he was in high school."

"It's against the law. You have rights."

"I did my part, you know? I'm not innocent."

"But you are. You're a child."

She smiled. "That's what you've been thinking about me all this time?"

"I can help you. Don't do anything drastic. Just come back next week and we'll figure it out."

We both heard Dorothy's footsteps on the stairs.

I said, "Promise you'll come back, and we'll decide what to do. You and me. Don't tell anyone else. This is between us."

She cocked her head. "Why do you care so much?"

"Why did you tell me?"

She smiled. "Because I knew you'd care."

Dorothy opened the door. "Is the lesson over? I have to get supper on the stove."

Hallie grabbed her violin case. I followed them and stood at the top of the stairs.

I had a feeling, in that moment, that I was releasing her from all of her pain. I knew I was participating in a sin, but I was taking it upon myself to explain. My mother had convinced me that no transgression would go undiscovered. "Be sure your sins will find you out," she used to say. "If you lie down with dogs, you're going to get up with fleas." I remembered all those warnings, but only lately had they seemed true. I was taking it upon myself to argue for Hallie and myself. I would say to God, Did you hear her play? Did you?

"Come back next week," I said.

"Okay," Hallie said.

"I can help you."

Dorothy turned. "With what?"

"She's just having some trouble with the bowing," I said.

"Oh, you musicians. The things you worry about."

11

Franklin fires Clive on a Monday, two weeks before Christmas. He does it at the beginning of the day rather than the end. He tells him in front of Patrick and Ernest and Declan. Other than that, he handles it perfectly.

I come in on the tail end of the commotion. Clive is yelling something about how no one in this godforsaken place knows a damn thing about music, and it's just fine with him, because now he can really pursue his career, and he's going to call all his students and tell them to take private lessons from him, never to set foot in McCoy's again. Patrick and Ernest are watching with neutral expressions. Declan is the only one who seems vaguely interested, scratching his long beard, his brow knitted with concern, as if he were the final arbiter, as if he were God.

He does kind of look like God, I find

myself thinking. I'm oblivious to Clive's ranting. I'm not sure why.

Clive finishes up his angry parting speech and nearly bumps into me as he turns to make his dramatic exit. He stares hard at me.

"You're in on this, too?"

"I'm not in on anything. I haven't even punched my time card."

"It was nice knowing you," he says.

The chimes rattle manically as he slams the door.

"Well, that is what we call that," Declan says. Then he gets to work on repairing a lute.

Franklin shudders as if caught by a sudden draft. He looks at me, then at Patrick and Ernest.

"Had to be done," he says.

Ernest just shrugs, to indicate his lack of involvement.

Patrick says, "Why?"

"He was bad for the shop," Franklin says.

"He had a lot of students," Patrick says.

"It just had to be done, all right?" Franklin says crankily, a death look in his eyes. He has been very intense and angry since he abandoned the Trailer Park Rogues. He is playing in Jenny's band now. They are called Moonlight. He denies that he really belongs to the band, but I have caught him making up flyers, and he no longer talks to me about practicing or getting gigs.

I find my time card and punch in. The clunking sound reverberates in the quiet room. There is no other sound but some infernal squeaking and plunking as Declan restores the lute.

"So we're short a salesperson today," I say, taking my place behind the cash register.

"We'll manage. People are dying to work here," Franklin says. "I get a dozen applications a week."

"You'd better start sorting through them," I say. "It's two weeks before Christmas. We are going to be busy."

Franklin knows this, and as the realization dawns, he heads off toward the manager's office to start digging through applications.

"That was exciting," Ernest says. He picks up a Collings guitar and starts tuning it. Then he breaks into an Allman Brothers riff.

Patrick is staring hard at me. I look at him and say, "What?"

"It was a big mistake," he tells me.

"So? What do you want me to do about it?"

"Talk to him."

"Clive?"

"Franklin."

I laugh derisively, realizing that I sound a little bit demonic.

"Franklin doesn't listen to me."

"You're the only one he does listen to. If you hadn't been late, you could have stopped it," Patrick says.

The hair on the back of my neck goes up. "I'm not late. And I couldn't have stopped it. It's over now. Let's move on."

We move on. There's nothing left to do. And I can't help thinking, as I stay busy all day, selling guitar strings and picks and tambourines and lessons (a great gift idea!) to frantic shoppers, that if Dorothy and Hallie come back tomorrow, they will notice the difference, will feel the absence of Clive, will want to know what happened to him, will want some kind of explanation.

But they don't come back and aren't coming back, and neither is Clive, and I'm going to have to adjust to all these changes as if I were a grown-up.

When Hallie left, I wanted to sob on someone's shoulder, like a broken-hearted teenager. But I didn't. I kept it to myself. I said, Be a grown-up. Now I'm wondering if that was the right choice. Now I'm thinking a grown-up might acknowledge her pain and invite others into it. A grown-up might have fought harder.

But no, just no, I tell myself. The whole point of teaching is that students come into your life for a little window of time. Then they leave. They are supposed to leave. And maybe employees are supposed to leave, too. Just clock out, Leah had said.

Franklin stays hidden in his office all day. The rest of us muddle through, pretending nothing has changed.

Ho, ho, ho.

When I get to my car that night, Clive is waiting for me, leaning against my car, his arms crossed, staring at nothing. He doesn't have an instrument with him. It's just Clive, just a moderately handsome twenty-eight-year-old with nowhere to go. He watches me with a crooked smile, as if we are long-lost lovers, discovering each other after years of imposed estrangement.

"How was work?" he asks.

"Clive, I'm sorry."

He shrugs. "Maybe it's for the best."

"You think so?"

His smile fades. His anger bursts through, surfacing first in his eyes, then in his mouth, which is pinched against the vitriol he wants to spew forth.

He says, "It's bullshit and you know it.

Franklin fired me because he hates bass players. I could sue him."

"Yes, you could. Using the discrimination against bass players clause of the Constitution."

"I'm glad you think it's so funny."

"I don't think it's funny. Do you need a ride?"

"Yes," he says.

I let him into my tired Honda. It's cold inside. I turn on the heater and the radio. Both are slow getting going. The radio is full of Christmas songs. It takes forever to find an agnostic station that plays the Smashing Pumpkins and Joy Division. Clive looks out the passenger window as I drive down Pico.

"Tell me where to turn," I suggest.

"Keep going," he says.

We hit the beach. He still doesn't tell me where to turn.

"Where do you live?" I ask.

"I don't want to go there."

"Where do you want to go?"

"Home with you," he says. "I just want to talk."

"Okay."

I take him to the trailer park. He doesn't seem surprised by it. Even as we get out of the car and head to my trailer, he just looks at his feet and grumbles under his breath.

"This is where I live," I say, unlocking the door to my trailer.

"Fine by me."

"You're coming in?"

"I just want a drink or something. Then I'll call a cab."

We go inside and he notices nothing. I tell him to sit down, and then I open a couple of beers for us. He sits in one of my two chairs and continues to stare at nothing in particular. I sip my beer, waiting. He holds his, staring.

Finally he says, "How can you stand it there?"

I shrug. "It's just my job."

He says, "What will I tell my students?"

"Whatever you want to."

"I like some of them, you know. I don't want to leave them."

"Then tell them to come with you."

He finally sips his beer and says, "What did you say to Hallie?"

I feel cold suddenly.

"I didn't tell her anything. She just . . . stopped coming."

"Why?"

I shrugged, trying to appear casual. "Students stop coming. It's what they do."

"But you really liked her. You thought she

193

was good."

"What was I supposed to do? Get a warrant for her arrest? She lost interest."

Clive looks sad for a moment, then stands, sighs, and sits by me on the couch. I feel every nerve in my body shut down, then come back to life, then shut down again. He is wearing a long-sleeved surfer-type T-shirt and jeans. His hair is short beyond logic, and the goatee on his chin looks like orphaned lint. His six earrings glint under the harsh overhead light. He is younger than I imagined, and I feel nothing for him except that my heart is racing and I feel dizzy.

Leah said it was okay. She didn't say it was inevitable.

He says, "Pearl, you're better than all of them put together. I've heard you play. Why do you put up with it? Why are you there?"

"I'm making a living. How else can I pay for my palatial estate?"

"You can start a band."

I laugh. "Violin players don't start bands."

"Why not? You've got violin, you've got me on bass. Those are the hardest instruments to find."

"I don't want to be in a band," I tell him, and it's true. I never really wanted to be in Franklin's band, either. I just wanted to be near him. But he wants to be near someone else. I've played that tune before.

Clive says, "Well, if you don't want to be in a band, what do you want to do?"

I shrug and admit the truth before I can stop myself. "I try not to want things."

He is taken aback by this because he is young and therefore he is all want.

"Well, that's just crazy. When you stop wanting things, you die," he says.

"Maybe not. Maybe when you stop wanting things, you figure out how to live."

I have no evidence of this, but I like the idea.

He is agitated. He shifts in his seat. He says, "What takes the place of want?"

I shrug again. "I don't know yet. I haven't been doing this for very long."

He moves away from me slightly and starts twisting his bottom lip between his fingers. Then he says, "You know what I read once?"

I sigh. I want to say, No, I don't give a shit what you read once. But I am polite and I have not given up on the idea of sleeping with him.

"What?" I say dutifully.

"That human beings are just mimics."

"Mimics?"

"Yeah. That everything we do is just an

imitation of what we've seen other people do. Like there's no original thought."

"That can't be true."

"Why not?" he asks, looking relieved. Because he doesn't want it to be true. Who would?

"Beethoven, Mozart, Mahler, to name a few. Isaac Newton, Albert Einstein. They broke the rules. They had original ideas."

"But this book I read says that breaking the rules is just a form of mimicking. They broke the rules because they saw someone else do it."

"I don't believe that," I say. "There has to be an original rule breaker."

I'm not actually sure, but I want to keep the argument alive. I am adding wood chips to the fire.

Clive gets excited by my resistance. He sits up straighter and says, "No, listen. In nature, there are all these organisms that imitate other things. There are bugs that look like sticks. Fish that look like rocks. Birds that look like leaves."

I nod, stifling a yawn. Yawns, I read once, are evidence of being overwhelmed rather than bored or exhausted. "Polar bears are white so that they blend into the snowy landscape. That's evolution. That's survival."

Clive says, "Mocking birds mimic other birds. They don't have a song of their own."

"Right, but the birds they mimic have songs of their own."

He scratches his goatee. I can see all the pistons firing in his brain. Me, I'm casting glances at my watch. I need to get some sleep or I will be cranky in the morning.

"So it figures," young Clive says, "that people behave that way, too. There are people who are put on earth to mimic other people. But I don't want to do that. I want to be original."

"The mystery of fingerprints and all that."

"What does that prove?"

"Originality."

"Oh, yeah," he says.

"And everybody mimics to a certain degree."

"Yeah," he says. "Like Franklin and Ernest. They aren't really original musicians. They don't write music. They play covers. They just mimic their heroes."

"Right."

"But you," he says, casting a dreamy-eyed look in my direction, "you don't mimic anyone."

"Sure, I do."

"Who?"

"Well, it's not really a who. It's a what."

"What, then?"

I know. Immediately I know. It comes to me, like a vision, but slower. It's a sound, a voice in my head. And what it says is, You are mimicking a musician. Because you aren't a musician. You are a teacher.

I don't say that out loud. Instead I turn to him and look at him and I wait. Because I know he will kiss me. And he does. And then things occur. The two of us confront each other.

We mimic lovers.

Clive gets up early, just as it is getting light outside. He dresses while I am still dozing in bed. He doesn't say anything. No one mentions coffee.

I lean up on an elbow and watch him. He looks so young, standing there, ready to depart. He is grinning, as if he's gotten away with something. But he hasn't gotten away with anything at all. He has to contend with me now, with that connection, however slim, that we have forged. As he stares at me, I see his smile start to fade. He knows he's gotten more than he bargained for. And he knows, looking at me, that I've gotten less. He wants me to grin back and say something like, Wow. But seeing him want it makes me determined not to give it. This could be a character flaw, or it could be a woman's natural reaction when a man thinks he's done all the work.

"I guess there's a silver lining to everything," he says. "Even getting fired."

The trouble with young men is that sooner or later, they say something young. And you can't wretch or even make a face. It's not polite.

"You'll find another job."

He says, "Maybe you could talk to Franklin?"

I laugh. "Oh. Was that some kind of down payment?"

He pretends to look hurt. "No. What are you talking about? No, of course not."

"It won't help," I tell him.

"What?"

"Talking to him. He doesn't listen to me."

"Okay. Whatever."

He opens the door, and more sunlight spills in. I feel nervous.

And I hear myself say, "When will I see you again?"

It's the death knell. It's a dirge.

He says, "You have my number. It's on the roster at McCoy's."

I want to say . . . what? Everything. I want to say, Come back here. You can't do this. Women don't chase men; men chase women. Don't run from the natural order of things.

I want to say, You can't do that to people. You can't do that to people of my gender. We invest, I want to say, in every physical transaction. What I've given you is worth more than a favor.

Except that in his mind, it isn't. And that's just a function of age. Sex is cheap when you're young. Disposable income. When you're older, it's a rare, mysterious metal.

He actually winks at me, then goes out and closes the door hard behind him.

I think of Hallie. I think of me saying, "Get rid of it."

As if our mistakes could be so neatly wiped away.

As if admitting we are wrong buys us anything.

It wasn't the pregnancy that made Hallie go away. Not directly.

The pregnancy itself went away, and I wasn't sure how. She wouldn't tell me.

I waited until the end of the lesson to ask so it wouldn't look as if I were some kind of obsessed old maid living vicariously through her sexual drama.

The lesson had gone well. She was play-ing with much more fire. She was concentrating and finding surprises and even smiling as she moved through the changes. I wondered if it was her secret, all along, that had been interfering with her music.

"So what are we going to do, Hallie?"

"Do about what?"

"What we talked about last time. Your problem."

She stared at me with genuine confusion. Then her eyebrows went up.

"Oh, that."

"Yes, that. I told you I'd help."

She waived a hand. "It's taken care of."

"What do you mean?"

"I took care of it."

"But how?"

"I know people. I have resources."

"Where did you get the money?"

She crossed her arms. "Don't you think that's a little bit none of your business?"

"You let me into this. Am I supposed to forget about it now?"

"Yes. You're supposed to forget about it now."

"I don't think that's possible."

She ignored me and started gathering her books.

"I think there's more to discuss." My tone was not lost on her. She turned her head to the side, the way dogs do when they hear a foreign sound.

"Like what?"

"Like why you were pregnant in the first place. Hallie, you have real talent and you must protect that. You're obligated to."

"Are you going to talk to me about God again?"

"I'm not talking about God. I'm talking about birth control."

"I know," she said. "I'll insist on it next time."

"There shouldn't be a next time. You shouldn't be having sex. You're too young."

"And you're too old."

This stole my breath a little, like a sudden wind. "For sex? Is that what you think?"

"No. To be talking to me about sex. You don't know what it's like to be my age."

"I've been your age."

"Not here, not now. It's different. Things are different."

"How are they different?"

"These are weird times, okay? And L.A. is a weird place. And you learn how to survive. You have reasons for doing things. You —"

"Are you talking about bargaining?"

Her smile faded, and she said, "I won't do it again, okay?"

"Hallie, did you make some kind of bargain? Because that's something else."

"You calling me a prostitute?"

"No. I don't think it was necessarily your choice."

She laughed. "How could it not be my choice? Do you even know how it works?"

"Yes, I know how it works. It's not an exchange of favors."

"What is it, then?"

I turned angry; I turned mean. I turned into your sour music teacher with the sour mothball breath.

I said, "It's a waste of my time to teach you if you're not going to take music seriously. If you're just farting around, I need to know so I can invest that energy somewhere else."

"I don't care what you do with your energy," she said without a hint of rancor.

For once in my life, I thought about what to say. I thought about it for as long as I believe I'm capable of. Here's what I came up with: Let's practice the Bach piece again, from the top, and this time I'm not going to help at all. I'm just going to listen."

So I listened, but I was far too angry to hear anything. They were just notes on a scale, coming forth, retreating, hiding, reappearing. The music was running away from her, and from me, and the two of us just sat in our folding metal chairs and watched it go. As if it weren't sacred. As if we could call it back, like a stubborn pet, and it would come back of its own volition.

We were relying on the wobbly truth that nothing likes to be kept out in the cold.

12

On Christmas Eve, I go down to Rae's for dinner. Rae's is a coffeeshop near McCoy's where most of us go to lunch when we forget to pack something. It's dirt cheap, but it still offends the money-conscious person to pay for a meal when you can bring a ham sandwich from home. On this particular night, I decide to go there as a treat to myself. It's too depressing to be in my trailer. Ralph, the drunk next door, has already come by for his free beer, and after he leaves, I am alone with the sounds of families preparing to be happy or else, goddamn it. I'm fully aware that on Christmas Day, somewhere in the late afternoon, unhappiness sets in as the kids tire of their toys and the parents tire of their children and each other, and the yelling starts, in the key of B. I know that is in store for me, so this is the last chance to relax.

I didn't always hate Christmas Eve. I used

to like it. Mark and I celebrated the holiday in big fashion. We spent money we didn't have on presents for each other, creating an elaborate system of hiding things. Christmas morning was always a treasure hunt. We wrapped up boxes, but in the boxes were little slips of paper, giving clues as to where to search for the presents. It took half a day to go through the ritual, and by late afternoon, when all the presents had been found, we'd start drinking mimosas and I'd start cooking. By nightfall we were exhausted and we'd collapse on the couch, curled up next to each other, still drinking but now watching silly news shows on the television. We'd always reserve enough energy to make love before going to bed. To hear me tell it, it was perfect.

Well, it was perfect in the early days, and I should have known better than to trust it. I should have worked at protecting it. I can safely say that our marriage began its decline the year we didn't hide each other's presents. We just bought stuff and wrapped it up and put it under the tree. It wasn't my idea; it was Mark's. He said, "It's getting a little old, isn't it, this treasure hunt?"

"Yeah, it's old," I said, unsure of myself, scared that my childishness was starting to turn him away. Sometimes I blame myself in this regard. I tell myself that nothing would have gone wrong if I had had the guts to say, No, this is what we do. This is part of our marriage. We're hiding our presents.

Deep down, I know that he had left me in his head long before he stopped hiding the presents. His insistence on a "normal" Christmas was just a symptom of his desire to wander. He didn't need to keep a magical Christmas with me, as he had found his own magic in the arms (or at least the adoring eyes) of a weepy coed.

But think, think, I tell myself on this Christmas Eve. There must have been a point where he started to lose interest, just a little bit. A point where you could have turned it around. The other half of my brain says, No matter. You don't want him anymore. No, not anymore, but the way he was then, the way we were then. I wanted that forever. If you really wanted it forever, you would have fought. Why didn't you fight?

Because, I say, after I have parked and started my walk to Rae's, we were always working too hard at happiness. Why did we hide our presents? Because in the early days, we had nothing to give. We were too poor. We bought each other cheap presents. We hid them in order to provide a sense of occasion. He bought me violin strings, and

CDs on sale, and secondhand jewelry. I bought him used books and computer paper and flimsy journals. Once, I gave him coupons to a car wash, and another time he gave me a box full of thread and needles. One year my big gift was a bottle of balsamic vinegar, because I liked it and it was too expensive. The same year, I gave him a silver pen, which he put in a drawer and never used.

If you want to, if you're interested, you can trace the demise of our marriage through the elevation of our Christmas gifts to each other. Once we stopped hiding the presents, once we started trying to make up for the lack of intrigue by paying more for the gifts, everything started going downhill.

The last Christmas we were together, we bought very nice things for each other. I got him a first edition of Robert Graves's *Goodbye to All That.* He got me a gold charm bracelet with musical instruments on it. Which was fine, but then we veered off into generic niceness. I bought him, that year, a cashmere scarf and leather gloves, and he bought me a sapphire ring. He never wore scarves or gloves, and I never wore fine jewelry. We had crossed over into that dangerous land of not knowing each other at all. We had crossed over into that dangerous land of letting the money speak. And once the money starts speaking, you tend to shut up.

I sit down at the counter at Rae's and am immediately waited on by Gloria, the waitress who is always there, always moderately cranky, always wearing too much makeup, her platinum hair piled up on her head. She has to be sixty, but she has devoted herself to denying the ravages of time. The only reason she hasn't had any work done is that she can't afford it. She talks to me about the recent advances in plastic surgery whenever I see her. She says, "Now they can make your lines go away with a laser. I'm thinking of doing that." I say, "No, don't do that. There has to be a downside." She also talks to me about diets, though she never seems motivated to go on one. She says, "Now there is this diet where you eat nothing but meat for thirty days. My next-door neighbor lost fifteen pounds."

Gloria never tries these things, but she never loses interest in talking about them.

When she sees me, she sidles up and says, "Merry Christmas. You want the fried egg sandwich?"

"No, I'm going to try the meat loaf."

"It's pretty good," she admits, jotting it down. "What the hell are you doing all alone on a night like this?"

"I'm always alone at Christmas," I tell her.

She rolls her dark eyes and says, "You're lucky. I've got four kids. Two of my own, two of my husband's. Tomorrow is going to be hell. Somebody is going to start screaming by ten o'clock. I can't wait till they leave home."

"Don't say that," I offer mildly, not meaning it.

She says, "Honey, if you only knew. Christmas is all about the children, and they never let you forget it. My feet hurt so bad, I'm thinking of asking my doctor to cut them off. How bad can a wheelchair be? People have to push you places. Sounds good to me."

"You don't mean that," I tell her. Gloria is a diabetic, and I realize that the eventuality of having her limbs cut off is in the proverbial cards.

People who get sick do it for a reason, I figure. And if you want someone to push you around in a wheelchair, you must have a sound purpose. Gloria is tired, and I can see where the idea of being pushed around might appeal to her. But those of us who eat at Rae's don't want to reckon with that just yet.

"I'll get your meat loaf," she says, sounding exhausted. "Anything else?"

"Just some iced tea."

"No problem," she says, moving away.

I am reading the print on the back of a Tabasco bottle when I hear my name.

"Pearl," the voice says.

I look up. Patrick is sitting not far down the counter, eating a hamburger.

I feel embarrassed and annoyed. I don't want to see anyone from work here. Not on Christmas Eve, when I'm supposed to be on vacation.

"What brings you here?" he asks.

I shrug, embarrassed, wanting to invent a story, but at the same time wanting to tell the truth. I strike a compromise.

I say, "I have some parties to go to. Thought it might be smart to eat first."

Patrick smiles. He says, "Yeah, I have some parties, too. It's always smart to eat."

I stifle a yawn, then say, "Where are your parties?"

He says, "Where are yours?"

"Here in Santa Monica," I answer quickly. It's true that I've been invited. Clive asked me to a party down in Venice, and my next-door neighbor asked me over for drinks. I declined both invitations. No need for him to know about that.

Gloria brings my meat loaf. She shoots a

look at Patrick and says, "Now, don't make trouble."

"You know I wouldn't," he tells her, and smiles at me.

I start eating my meat loaf, hoping he'll ignore me, but he doesn't. He is staring at me. He eventually moves down a couple of seats till he is two seats away from me.

He leans toward me and says, "I have to go to a party, and I don't want to go alone. How would you feel about going with me?"

"I'd feel cranky," I say, biting into the meat loaf. It's good, and I know I'd feel a lot less cranky if I could be left alone.

Patrick says, "I live in Venice. In a loft near the beach. This party is close to my house. I could drive us. I could drive you home. I just don't want to go by myself."

Keep in mind that all of these sentences are laced with his particular speech impediment, the *s*'s sounding like *sh*'s.

The meat loaf is really good, so I feel happy and comfortable enough to say, "Patrick, I just want to eat, and then I want to go home and go to bed."

He smiles. His eyes are a brighter blue than I had imagined. I am remembering Clive's eyes and thinking that if they were as piercing and sincere as Patrick's, the subsequent morning would not have ended so badly.

But this is a dangerous thing to think.

Patrick says, "Just come with me to this party. I'll drive you home. What do you say?"

"I'd say you are relentless."

He grins. He says, "That might be the nicest thing anyone has ever said about me."

I know I am going with him. I just don't know what it means.

The party is at someone's house on one of the Venice canals. What most people know about Venice Beach is its history of crime, wackiness, and weirdos. They know about Muscle Beach, that bizarre stretch of sand where the denizens of the Sun Belt come to show off their peculiar talents. Weight lifters, fire-eaters, break-dancers, in-line skaters, human mannequins, chain-saw jugglers — the list goes on. It is the place you take visitors from out of town, ostensibly to show them the local color, but secretly (I believe) to discourage them from moving here. It usually works. People leave Venice shaking their heads, laughing and amazed but a little bit sick to their stomachs, the way you feel leaving any circus. A little taste of freakiness goes a long way.

Not many people, even the ones who live in L.A., know about the Venice canals. The city itself was built in homage, as it were, to the real Venice, and in true Los Angeles fashion, the developer (a Mr. Abbot Kinney, I'm told) culled everything that was bad about the original city and omitted the good. The bad being an impractical array of houses on unstable land, surrounded by vaguely smelly and polluted waters. The good being excellent Italian cuisine, hundreds of years of architectural superiority, a profitable glass factory, and a link to the European continent.

That is my jaded view of the Venice canals, but the truth is, they are reasonably quaint and romantic, particularly at night, when the murky waters are invisible and the Craftsman-style houses are softly lit. The sound of the water lapping against the sidewalks is soothing, and on this particular night, Christmas Eve, the atmosphere is almost magical, with a tasteful display of white Christmas lights linking the houses in a common theme. It is almost breathtaking.

Patrick leads me to one of the nicer houses on the block, which is full of happy people holding festive drinks, talking in moderate tones, laughing, and clapping one another on the back. The house is lit mostly by candles, and an enormous Christmas tree takes up most of the living room. Classical

Christmas carols are playing softly on the stereo, and as soon as I walk in, I never want to leave. I want to be friends with every person in this house, and they seem to want to be friends with me, too. Patrick introduces me as Pearl, giving no explanation as to how he knows me (leaving us open to speculation that we're a couple, I'm thinking), and goes off to get me a drink. No one asks me what I do for a living; nor do they offer such information about themselves. Which might not seem so strange to an outsider, but in Los Angeles, what you do for a living is everything.

I've engaged in half a dozen conversations before Patrick returns. I've talked to a pleasant man named Gerald, who seems to be Austrian or German, and his attractive girlfriend, Lucia, who seems to be not Austrian or German, and I've talked to a large, funny woman named Justine, who revealed to me that she's recently divorced and this is her first Christmas alone, but it's not so bad. I've talked to a large, bearded man named Toby, who offered a positive dissertation on the NFL, and I've talked to a quiet blond Englishwoman with a baby on her hip. The woman is named Rosemary; the baby is named Imogen. They both seem to live here, and Rosemary is worried that the eggnog is not up to snuff. Excusing herself and her baby, she goes off in search of a man named Simon. This is when Patrick returns, offering me a glass of white wine. I accept it gratefully.

He clinks glasses with me (he's drinking an amber-colored drink on ice) and says, "Merry Christmas."

"How do you know these people?" I ask.

"From my former life," he says enigmatically.

"What former life?"

"When I was a teacher. Simon and I were in the same department."

"Where did you teach?"

"At UCLA," he says without much fanfare.

I feel a kind of jolt, the kind you feel when two entirely disparate worlds accidentally collide. When that happens, I feel that either God or the devil is at work, and I can't relax until I know which one.

"Do you know Mark Hooper?" I ask.

"No. What department is he in?"

"He's a history professor."

He shakes his head, with just a hint of disdain. "We didn't mix with those people."

"What department were you in?"

"Physics," he says.

I struggle to hide my reaction. He looks at

me, and as my reaction rises to the surface anyway, he looks away. Something in my expression bothers him. I think it must be disbelief.

"You're a physics teacher?"

"I was," he says.

"Why did you stop?"

He shrugs. "It made me crazy. Physics will do that to you."

"Well, how did you end up working in a music store?"

"It was a logical progression," he says.

"How is that?"

He shrugs, pausing to sip from his glass. "Music and physics are the same thing."

"Oh, really?"

"Yes, really." He laughs now, looking straight at me. "Pearl, no one knows that better than you."

"I don't know what you're talking about."

"Frequencies. Vibrations. Sound waves."

"Physics and music are connected. They aren't the same thing."

"What makes you say that?"

"One is a science."

He raises an eyebrow at me. "Which one?"

"Music is not a science."

"Prove it."

"I don't have to. I play it."

"So do I," he insists.

I decide not to challenge him. After all, he is a physics teacher. He knows stuff.

He's also a person with a life. This is his life I'm standing in, and it's bigger than mine, with more people in it. How did I let myself get so isolated? I wonder, but I know. I've always been isolated. It was a condition I was born with, like asthma or cerebral palsy. It was exacerbated by parents who were surprised and baffled by me. Some children, like Imogen, get to arrive on earth with this one simple assurance: You were invited, and you are welcome. Those of us who imposed our existence on a couple of angry and resistant participants spend most of our lives feeling sorry that we came. Wondering why we did come. And not knowing, we stand aside and try not to make a fuss.

Some of that dissipated when I met Mark. My abject nothingness went away when we got married. I am here to be a certain man's wife. That was enough of a thing to be, for many years. But when that went away, I had to find another purpose. When I started to work at McCoy's, I came to a better conclusion. I am here to work. I am here to teach people. There really is a place for me, after all.

Hallie became the strongest evidence of

that. And there were weeks, maybe even months, when I thought she was my whole reason for existence.

When she went away, I didn't know what to do.

I haven't known what to do for a long time.

Suddenly Patrick says, "Okay, here's the truth. I taught physics for eight years, and then I got involved in research. I was doing quite well with it, but . . . I don't know how to explain it, except to say that my brain overheated. It ran too hot, like a car engine. I had a little breakdown. I went away for a while. When I came back, I wanted to be around music. That's how I ended up at McCoy's."

"But what instrument do you play?" I ask, still stuck on that point. He just smiles at the ground, and I say, "You have to play something. Franklin doesn't hire people unless they can play something."

"I told you before," he says.

"Tell me again."

"I play them all," he says quietly. As if he wants it to remain a secret.

"What do you mean?" I ask, feeling a little desperate.

"Just that, Pearl. I hear them all, I play them all. I can pick up any instrument and play it. I don't know why or how. I've never had a lesson. I look at musical notation, and it makes sense to me. It's just math. Easy math, at that. In fact, music was one of the earliest scientific experiments — the realization that the length of a string determines its pitch. As far as the sounds are concerned, they are just waves, you know? They exist in certain frequencies, on certain planes. They are already out there. All you do on your violin is pull the waves out of the air and transform them from one dimension to another."

As Patrick is saying this, I've noticed that his strange lisp has gone away. He is speaking normally.

I say, "I think I do more than that when I play the violin."

"Of course you think so. But you're wrong. It's not magic. It's science."

I have no argument, so he goes on speaking. He says, "In quantum physics, there is this notion — this belief, I suppose — that we are all connected by a kind of ether. We're all in the same soup. There is a finite amount of energy on earth. We tap into it or we reject it. If you choose to reject it, you're like a free radical, bouncing off the walls, dividing and subdividing at will, creating illness and chaos. But if you accept the ether, if you accept that energy is finite, while still holding the paradoxical belief that space itself is infinite, then you are in striking distance of the truth. You can get a glimpse of the keys to the kingdom. You can't own the keys to the kingdom, but knowing they exist is almost the same. Do you understand?"

I say, "Wait a minute. Does the physics prove chaos or does it prove order?"

"It suggests both."

"It can't be both, Patrick. You have to pick."

"We can't prove either one. Einstein set out to prove the unified field theory. Order. His efforts to prove it resulted in the atom bomb. Chaos."

"All that means is that the answer hasn't been found. It doesn't mean there's no answer."

He looks at me, raising his chin in an authoritative gesture. "You tell me. Does your life have meaning?"

"That's a horrible question."

"Why? Don't you ever ask yourself that?"

"Sure."

"And the answer is?"

"Sometimes it does, sometimes it doesn't."

"No. All or nothing. Now you have to pick."

I can't pick. I'm too drunk. "Can't we just talk about the weather?" I ask.

"Sure," he says, smiling. "That's physics, too."

Patrick takes me back to my trailer. I am sitting close to the door in his car, a Volkswagen something, and I am staring out the window, wondering how I ended up here. I feel as if I've been abducted by an alien and taken to a place in another dimension. Tomorrow, when I tell people about this, they won't believe it. And Patrick will deny it.

Like Clive and Franklin, he has no real reaction to the fact that I live here. He walks me to the door. I fumble with my keys and open it. I wait for him to follow me in, but he doesn't.

I suppose I am feeling brave, because not long ago I had sex with a twenty-eight-year-old. Or maybe I am just feeling drunk, which I am. But I realize, standing there with Patrick, that it is going to be easy to have sex with him, because once you start, what's to stop you? Once you prove that sex has no real meaning, can't you just take it from anywhere? Isn't it all the same — a level playing field?

"Come in for a drink," I say.

He smiles. "I don't want a drink. Thanks."

"But can't you just . . . come in?"

"No," he says. "I don't want to do that."

"Why?" I ask defiantly. I can feel an anger bubbling up inside me, and it gives me comfort, as if I'm being reminded of who I am.

Patrick leans against the doorframe, looking quite harmless with his ponytail and his long, girly eyelashes. He says, "You're asking me to sleep with you."

"I'm not asking. I'm just saying, why don't you come in?"

He laughs because he knows there's no difference.

He is going to deny me, and because of this, I suddenly find him ridiculously attractive. I never noticed how straight his posture is, or how square his jaw, or how clean and flawless his skin. I never noticed that he has muscles and big hands.

Maybe that's why he's annoyed with me. Because I never noticed.

He doesn't move. He's waiting for me to say something.

I say, "Look, here we are, both alone on Christmas Eve. What difference does it make? Where's the harm in it?"

Staring at me with his clear blue eyes, not a hint of anything in them, like rancor or suspicion or interest, he says, "I'm not sure I like you."

This shocks me. I cannot speak for a second, and yet he waits. It would have been a perfect exit line, and yet he waits.

I say, "What do you mean, you don't like me? We just spent the evening together. We work together." When he has no reaction to this, I become a little desperate. I say, "Who are you kidding? I see the way you look at me."

"When?" he asks.

"At the shop," I answer.

"Oh, well. That's just admiration."

"Admiration?"

"Or maybe attraction?"

"You're attracted to me, you admire me, but you don't like me?"

"That happens," he says.

And I know it's true, so I want to say, in my defense, or in the defense of something abstract, some truism or philosophy, Since when does a man have to like a woman to sleep with her?

But I don't say that because I am far too hung up on this notion of not being liked by him.

So I say, "You're telling me that . . . what?

I'm not likable?"

"Maybe," he admits.

"What does it take?" I ask, hearing my voice rising an octave. "How does a person become likable?"

Now he straightens up, backing down my steps in the dark.

He thinks about it for what feels like a full minute.

"A person extends herself," he says.

"What? I'm not extended?"

"Good night, Pearl," he says, and walks toward his car.

"I extend myself all the time," I say weakly after him.

He gets into his car and slams the door. I watch the car backing out of the trailer park. I yell out, "At least I know what instrument I play!"

I watch his red taillights, still yelling after him: "Pick an instrument already, Patrick! Pick one and play it!"

There is nothing left but the dull sound of his car retreating, and the dust settling in front of my trailer, like tainted snow.

13

I turned on Hallie.

It hurts to admit it.

After the pregnancy, I turned on her.

I wasn't so obvious about it at first. It took the form of being hypercritical of her playing. She was hooked into the instrument by then, so I knew I could get away with it. Whenever she pointed out that I was being too hard on her, I fell back on the weak and tired explanation that I expected more from her. I did expect more from her. But not for her. I expected more for me. I was putting in the time. I was expending the energy. I wanted something back.

Then she started to miss some lessons. Not often, but it happened. It happens with all students. They have other events at school, or they have tests to study for, or they have family occasions. I usually make allowances. I made allowances for Hallie, too, in that I didn't fire her. But whenever she missed a lesson, I made her pay.

I liked making her pay. I was angry.

We fought often. I always won. She would try to tell me that it was hard getting time to play at her house, which I knew perfectly well it must be, but I said, "Look, if you want to be great, you can't keep throwing excuses at me." So she stopped throwing the excuses. Her heart was less and less in it. The music was leaking out of her, like air from a worn tire.

I was killing her. I had the power to do that. I felt the way my father must have felt, watching the flames engulf the only thing that I loved. It was captivating. The sense of power created a feeling of delirium. She needed me, but she did not respect me, so I could make her pay.

God, I hope that wasn't how it went, but I think it was. We could no longer connect. Once, when she was playing particularly well, she paused, put her instrument aside, and said, "Do you ever think of adopting anyone?"

I knew she meant herself.

I said, "I live alone. I don't have any money."

"So the answer is no."

I looked at her. She seemed so small, even in her dangerous black clothes, even with her eyebrow stud.

"Even if I were willing, I don't have any legal grounds."

"It's just bad there," she said to me, in a rare moment of confession. She usually kept things to herself. And I didn't mind. Part of me, the selfish part, didn't want to hear about her dire circumstances. I had seen them for myself. It was too painful to contemplate.

On the other hand, I told myself, it wasn't that bad. People had endured worse, I figured. And Hallie had talent, which was something she could lean on in times of distress. Some kids have nothing at all to hope for.

I said, "Hallie, we all have a cross to bear. My parents didn't want me, either. And they were my real parents. Your decision to move on and succeed is up to you. You can't ride the wave of your bad fortune forever."

She had no reaction to that. She just picked up her instrument and started playing again.

Meanwhile, I felt terrible about the way I was treating her. I wasn't sure why I couldn't recover from the perceived slight I had felt. So the kid got herself knocked up. Was she the first fourteen-year-old to do that? And was I responsible for it? Was I her surrogate mother?

I did extend myself to her. No matter what Patrick says, I am capable of extending myself. I tried to help her. She rejected my wisdom and my guidance. She just wanted the quick fix. This was why I resented her.

My relationship with her was becoming torturous. I dreaded her lessons and looked forward to them; I loved her and despised her. We were entwined in some disturbing paradox, and it was in our sessions that the darkness and the light met in the middle and blotted each other out.

Like fire on fire.

It was the first week in September, a little less than a year after we'd met, when everything came to a head.

The Santa Ana winds were blowing, which made the air around us unseasonably hot and dry. The Santa Anas were known as the devil winds. Raymond Chandler wrote about them. He claimed they caused people to kill one another. Everyone grew restless; the air was so dry and full of static, you had the sense that one lone match could set the world ablaze.

My allergies were acting up, and I was cranky. Hallie was cranky, too. We attempted the first piece of sheet music, and when she messed it up, I told her to play the scales.

She did it, almost out of habit. Her right wrist was stiff, and she was screeching the notes, which hurt my ears. I grabbed her wrist to loosen it, but she must have thought I was going to hit her, so she threw down the instrument and backed into a corner, screaming, "Leave me alone!"

Her voice must have been exceptionally loud, because Franklin tapped on the door and said, "Everything all right in there?"

I cracked it and said, "Everything is fine."

He raised an eyebrow at me, and I smiled. He went away.

After I closed the door, I turned back to Hallie and said, "What is wrong with you?"

She stood up straight, looked me in the eye, and said, "I want to quit."

I had been waiting for those words. I had been expecting them, maybe even forcing them. Here they were, and I had no idea what to do with them.

The Santa Anas were howling. A window blew open and banged hard against the wall. Hallie jumped and shrank deeper into herself and into her corner. I crossed the room and closed the window, suddenly feeling calm and cold. It was only wind. It was only a child. It was only music.

I walked back toward her without speaking. I sat down in my metal folding chair and said, "Well, what are we going to do about that?"

She shrugged and embarked on biting her hangnails.

"I can't stop you, of course," I said.

She remained silent.

"I think you'd be throwing away an immense amount of talent."

"What do you care?" she responded.

"I hate to see talent go to waste."

"So if I weren't talented, you wouldn't care?" she said. "If I weren't talented, you'd be fine with seeing me go to waste?"

I wasn't sure how to reply. I hadn't thought about it. But I took a moment to do just that, and it worried me when I realized it might actually be true. I had never seen Hallie as a person apart from her talent. It was possible I had never truly cared about her.

I shook my head, looking at the stained carpet. No, that couldn't be the case. I had other talented kids. Rosamund, for example. She was probably just as talented and had more time to develop the talent. She had an equally disturbed home life, on an entirely different scale, but I didn't spend much free time thinking about her. Hallie filled my thoughts all the time. I even dreamed about her. I was connected to her in a way that frightened me. But the incident with the pregnancy had caused me to distance myself. I was afraid of getting hurt.

And that is pathetic, I remember thinking. You are protecting yourself from getting involved with a child. As if that kind of hurt could equal what you felt when Mark left. As if there were no hierarchy of pain.

I felt humbled in that moment, so I looked up at her and said, "I just think you should keep playing, Hallie."

Some element of defiance, or hope, then leaked out of her face, and she walked back to her chair and sat down. She looked at her knees; one of them was peeking out of a hole in her jeans.

"I won't quit playing," she said. "But I don't want to take lessons from you anymore."

Not long before Mark left me for Stephanie, he stopped having sex with me. I didn't know about Stephanie then. I thought I was doing something wrong. So I tried to be sexy. I made trips to Victoria's Secret. I had more black lace than a Portuguese widow. One night I told Mark I was going to bed, and that I would wait up for him. This was our code. I put on something from the call-girl collection and waited. An hour went by. I dozed off and woke up again. I got up to see what Mark was doing, and I found him in the den, watching a bad Arnold Schwarzenegger movie on TV. Not so much watching it as staring blankly. He was avoiding coming to bed. He was avoiding having sex with me. And I realized in that moment, Oh, it's not that he doesn't *want* me. It's that he doesn't want *me.*

Hallie still wanted music. She just didn't want it from me.

Anger crept up from wherever it lived inside me and settled in my face. I was sure it was bright red. I was sure Hallie could see it.

"Well, then you should go find another teacher," I said.

She nodded and started packing up her instrument.

"I don't know where you're going to find someone," I said.

"Lots of people teach violin."

"Not for these prices," I told her. "McCoy's is as cheap as you'll find. I'm the best you can get for this money."

She shrugged. "So I'll pay more."

"You will?"

"Yeah."

"Your father doesn't even want to pay my fee."

She said nothing.

"You had to fight to keep coming here. Do you really think they are going to go to the trouble of finding another teacher, and pay more?"

"I'll get him to pay," she said.

"How?" I asked, feeling mean.

"I just will."

She grabbed her violin case and walked out. I should have left it at that. I should have stayed in the musty little room and waited for my next student. But I couldn't. I followed her.

She had stormed out of McCoy's without warning her mother. Dorothy had remained behind, no doubt engaging Ernest or Franklin in some discussion of guitars or money. Hallie was hurrying down the sidewalk, the hot wind whipping through her short black hair. Trash was gusting around in the gutters. There was an eerie sort of moan on the street. It felt like the end of the world.

"Hallie, be reasonable," I said. "You won't get him to pay. If you leave me, music will be over for you."

"I'll get him to pay," she said, not looking back at me.

"How?"

"I know how."

"What will you do? Say please? He doesn't like music."

It was a cheap shot, but I felt desperate. She stopped and turned to me, clutching her violin case next to her chest.

"Yeah, but he likes me," she said.

The world around us suddenly turned silent. Or maybe it just turned silent for me. I couldn't hear the cars on Pico. I couldn't hear the wind. My ears just quit working, which is what happens, I'm told, when you hear something you don't want to hear.

She said, "We have a deal, him and me."

"Hallie," I said quietly. Or I thought I said it. I could no longer hear my own voice. All I could hear was the relentless devil wind, like a thousand wailing souls in purgatory.

"You're the one who said it was worth anything," she reminded me.

And she left me with that to think about for a while. Days, months, or the rest of my life.

It was easy, really, what came next. I wondered why I had made it so hard.

From Franklin's office I called Leah at work and asked for that name. The name of the social worker. She said, "Are you sure?" and I was sure.

I called the social worker. She listened. She asked questions. She said they would look into it.

I hung up the phone and I felt it rise up,

terrible and real, that feeling I'd had when I saw the violin burning on the leaves and I knew something deep inside me had changed and it would take a long time to know what.

14

America is a hard country, full of hard people.

It is amusing that anyone anywhere thinks of us as being soft and spoiled, privileged, lazy, unchallenged, or indifferent, pickled with happiness.

My father used to say that kind of thing to me, and I let his rants drift by my ears, preoccupied, as I was, with my own inalienable rights. I thought he was talking about himself, his own experience with extreme poverty, forced service in the Korean War, and a disappointing adult life full of things he did not ask for and did not understand. But as I grew older, I realized he was referring to something much bigger than I could ever grasp. Something bigger than his own personal history, bigger than the Depression, World War II, and polio. Bigger than his angry marriage and his obsession with fire, his need to conform and his wild desire to break the same rules he constructed and held dear.

I went through a phase in my life, my freshman year in college, when I became obsessed with reading biographies. I was hungry for the stories of other people's lives. I was comparing them, I suppose, to my own, with a frantic desire to determine whether I had fared better or worse, whether I could learn from their failures and emulate their successes. I wasn't sure what I was looking for. I just wanted to know.

I started with the biographies of musicians — Hank Williams, Woody Guthrie, Elvis Presley, Patsy Cline, Robert Johnson, Johnny Cash, Jerry Lee Lewis, Sam Cooke. I enjoyed the early years especially, the chapters that described their humble beginnings, during which time there was no reason to suspect that these people would amount to anything at all. In most cases it seemed these people were destined either for obscurity or for a life of crime. They were as surprised as anyone when things took a turn for the better. I skimmed the successful years, then got interested again in the long decline. One could argue that I was interested only in the bad news. But it was more serious than that. I was interested in the demons that haunted, it seemed to me, every living person. Certainly every person who had ever ventured into music.

It was clear how God felt about musicians. He kept killing them off, mostly in small planes.

My curiosity grew, and I started reading biographies of writers, politicians, dancers, generals, scientists. After a while it didn't matter what the person had done to distinguish himself. I had discovered that every person had a story, and I wanted to know them all.

I read about Edgar Allen Poe, Thomas Jefferson, Cole Porter, Daphne du Maurier, Diane Arbus, John Fante, Albert Einstein, Grace Kelly, Martin Luther, Meister Eckehart, Gelsey Kirkland, Isaac Newton, Edgar Cayce, Helen Keller, Mark Twain, Dorothy Parker, John Brown, Robert E. Lee, Picasso, Jung, William Faulkner, and William Shakespeare. I didn't have to be interested in the person's work at all. In fact, I didn't care if the person had done anything of importance. I could have read the biography of my next-door neighbor, if it had been written in a true and dramatic style.

I loved stories of people. They were born to such and such parents, in such and such a place. They dealt with this hardship and the other. They had a childhood illness.

They rescued someone from death. They turned to crime, away from crime. They nearly died, came back to life, worshipped God or the devil. They were happy, unhappy, successful, unsuccessful. Fell in love, out of love, were loyal, betrayed people, betrayed themselves, longed for something, got it or didn't get it, and in the end, they died.

I was interested, I suppose, in the jagged nature of any person's life. I was looking, I also suppose, for that time line, that linear path resulting in logic and satisfaction. However, I am fairly certain that if I had found it, I would have been disappointed. What intrigued me, even thrilled me in some dark way, was that none of these lives made any kind of sense. Every life seemed incomplete. Every life seemed random in its trajectory, contradictory in its purpose.

I liked that.

Any mediocre psychologist would say that I was filled with schadenfreude, or the desire to see others fail. That I was looking for something to justify my own emptiness, my own suspicion that my life had no real design, no clear purpose. But I don't think so. That is too easy. I was looking, I think, for some evidence that a life is not supposed to have such obvious boundaries, such a clear narrative. Therefore it is really all right to feel completely lost inside your own circumstances. That we all arrive here disconnected and disconcerted and we just do the best we can, hitting and missing. Hitting more than missing, if we are lucky. And then, because God is merciful, it eventually stops.

It was through reading these biographies that I was eventually able to forgive my parents, then to forgive myself. Because we are all just feeling our way through the dark, I told myself in my biography days. There are just as many fascinating stories that are never told, because the person never got anything published, produced, recorded, awarded, or photographed. But these biographies were the proof I needed that no life really falls into place.

When I first moved to California, I forgot about the biographies, and my biography phase, because it seemed to me that life in Los Angeles defied that logic. I felt I was surrounded by people who knew exactly what they were doing. They knew where they had been and where they were heading, and anyone without a similar knowledge was left out in the cold. I didn't mind being in the cold so much. But it was a paradigm shift for me. I went from believing that no one has the answers, to thinking that every-one has the answers but me.

After Hallie left, I started reading biogra-phies again. I had to be reminded. I needed to know my part in her story. In any given biography, I show up around chapter twelve. I am the person who could have made a difference but didn't. I am the person who met her at the crossroads of her life, gave her a little bit of helpful information, then let her down. I am the person who, when you get to this particular chapter in her biography, makes the reader shake his head and say, "Oh, well, that's the one who let her get away. That is the turning point right there."

But the thing that strikes me about these biographies, then and now, are the pictures. I loved the pictures most of all. In most good biographies, hidden like little trea-sures, like golden Easter eggs in the middle of the book, are the pictures. The pictures begin at the beginning. The mother and father with their child, staring at the camera in homemade clothes, all stoic and satisfied, determined and ready to face the future. They don't realize, when the picture is taken, that they are holding some national treasure on their knee. The treasure himself (or herself) always appears detached, distanced, unrelated, ready to escape. You look at the pictures and you think, Well, no wonder. But it isn't fair. Any family photograph would reveal the rebellious child who has other things in mind. Very few of them go on to distinguish themselves. Yet in every photo, there is the one who wants to get away.

And in the photo, this is how the parents look: tired, distracted, angry, compromised. Their eyes are dark and beady, their faces are thin and gaunt, or swollen, protruded, and defiant. In every picture the parent says, It was hard, getting here. It was so goddamn hard to arrive at this point. And no one will ever know. No one will ever know or care how hard it was to get here. You want a picture? I'll give you a picture. A picture might tell a thousand stories, but it will never tell mine.

America is a hard place, full of hard people.

That is what the picture says. Even when the story says something else.

The call came a month later.

Despite her threats, Hallie had been showing up for lessons, and we were keeping it all very professional. She didn't seem to be curious about my sudden lack of interest in her. She seemed to prefer it. She didn't talk about home, and her playing was improving.

I was too nervous to ask her anything. I didn't know if the social worker had stopped by or not. I didn't know if Social Services would involve her. I didn't know if she would associate it with me. I just waited for her to let me know what was going on. In the meantime, I focused on her bowing, her wrist, the notes. It surprised me that she didn't detect the difference in me. And it made me wonder if she had ever really seen me at all.

I was just working in the store on a slow day, leafing through some trade magazine and checking my watch. I didn't have anywhere to go, but there were times when I just needed different walls. I needed not to hear the crazy commotion of instruments being moved and tried or the inane chatter of my colleagues.

Franklin called me into the office.

"Phone for you," he said.

"I could have taken it up front."

"I think it's serious," he said. "It's the police."

My heart pounded. Visions emerged of Mark and Stephanie strewn on the highway, and when it was real, I couldn't wish for it.

Couldn't believe I had ever pictured a demise. Wondered how I could have been so careless.

"Hello?" I asked in a shaky voice. Franklin stood by me, waiting.

The officer was calling from Santa Monica, and he wondered if I could come down to the station to speak about a matter concerning Hallie Bolaris. I asked if she was all right and he said that she was. But he wanted to ask me a few questions.

"Can I ask what it's regarding?"

"We can get into all that when you get here."

I wanted to ask more, but Franklin was standing there, watching me and waiting. I told the officer that I'd be right there.

I hung up the phone. My hand was visibly shaking.

"What's all that?" Franklin asked.

"He wouldn't really say. I think it has to do with some robberies in my neighborhood. I have to go in."

"Is who all right?" he asked.

"What?"

"You asked if she was all right. Who is she?"

"A neighbor. He says she's fine. Do you mind if I take off now?"

"Sure. You seem upset. Do you need me

to drive you?"

"No, I'll be fine."

"Pearl, I'd be happy to."

"Stop it. Stop being so concerned about me. I'm not as fragile as you think. Walking me to my car and all that. What's it about, Franklin? I've been alone a long time. I think I can handle it."

He looked wounded, and for the first time I realized he might actually care about me. Not in the way I hoped, but it was concern nonetheless, and I wasn't sure how I'd gotten to the point where another person's compassion made me feel so suspicious.

"I'm sorry," I said. "It's just unnerving to get a call from the police. I thought someone was dead."

"But nobody is?"

"Not yet," I said.

I drove without seeing the streets, and I didn't let myself imagine anything. I listened to the songs on the radio and for some reason I thought about my lost cat, Roy. I wasn't sure why except that I had let him go without much of a fight. I had let him get away. As I had let Mark get away. As I had hoped not to let Hallie get away. Los Angeles seemed stark and random as I navigated the streets. All the transients, all the people who didn't seem to belong to anyone — I always felt like one of them. Rootless, disconnected. It was strange, but being called in to see the police made me feel anchored somehow, suddenly part of a community.

I announced myself at the front desk, and soon a uniformed officer who seemed not much older than Clive came to greet me. He was prematurely bald and his eyes were round and jolly. He introduced himself as Officer Mulligan and he touched my elbow as he led me back to his desk. It felt formal and considerate, like a date at a cotillion.

I sat on a folding chair next to his desk, and I was vaguely aware of all the activity around me. I felt as if I was on a TV show.

He took down my name and address, and he was slow writing it. He asked me my birth date and where I was employed. I struggled against my impatience. Finally he put his pen down and sat back in his chair and told me what was going on.

Hallie Bolaris, he said, and her parents had been in earlier to file a complaint. In fact, they were still somewhere in the building, talking to a social worker. He wanted to disclose that, in case I ran into them. I asked what kind of complaint, and he scratched his bald head.

He said, "You realize, we're not accusing

you of anything. We just have to check out stuff like this."

"Stuff like what?"

He said, "It's delicate, Miss Swain."

"Just tell me."

So he told me. A social worker had gone out to visit the Edwards family on a tip that Hallie was being abused by someone in the family, most likely her adopted father. I could feel the blood racing in my veins. I was afraid and euphoric at the same time. I had set something in motion. I had made something happen. But the careful way Officer Mulligan was talking to me was a warning that it hadn't turned out as I imagined.

He said, "I'm not really supposed to disclose this, but the social worker couldn't find any evidence of abuse. After an exhaustive search, there was just nothing to support it. They interviewed everyone in the family, including Hallie, and they all thought the charge was preposterous. Everyone was upset by it, but Hallie was the most upset."

I said, "I imagine that's how it usually goes. I have a friend in family law. She says the victims often recant, sometimes in court."

"Yes, that does happen. But the social worker believed her, and she's trained to recognize things like that."

"Okay, but isn't my involvement confidential? How did they know it was me?"

"Maybe they knew, maybe they didn't. They suspected, let's call it. The thing is, Miss Swain, Hallie Bolaris claims that something else altogether occurred."

"What? What else?"

"Miss Bolaris claims that you took an unnatural interest in her."

My stomach knotted and I felt crazy. The last time I had felt that crazy was when I knew Mark was having an affair and he wouldn't admit it. His earnest protests had made me feel as if I were spinning a hysterical web of fantasy. But this was worse. So much worse because of the extremity of the lie and the fragility of the trust.

"Unnatural," I said.

"She claims that you convinced her she was being abused and that you encouraged her to leave her family and come live with you."

"Live with me? I live in a trailer. I don't even have room for a cat."

"The point is, she says you have become obsessed with her. She says you made certain gestures toward her."

My dread hardened into a pearl of anger, lodged in my chest. "Advances, you mean. Sexual advances."

"She stopped just short of saying that you did anything. Physically. More like you emotionally persuaded her."

Somehow I managed to override my fear and disappointment. I found the power in the anger that was now invading me and spreading through my body like a fever.

I managed not to give voice to the eruption. I calmly explained to Officer Mulligan that I had only cared about Hallie as a teacher. And that Hallie had confided in me, had as much as confessed that she was trading herself for music lessons. I told him about her pregnancy and how it had mysteriously gone away. I told him about her bruises and about my tense visit to the Edwardses' home. I told him about my obligation, as a teacher, to report any concerns that I had. I had concerns and I weighed them carefully and consulted a friend before I made the decision to call someone. It had been difficult, I told him, but I couldn't just stand by and do nothing.

Office Mulligan nodded with an understanding expression. Then he asked if I was married. I told him I didn't think it was relevant. He asked if I had a boyfriend, and I told him that was really not relevant and then I demanded to know if I was being charged with anything.

"No, not officially," he said. "But these are things you'll be asked eventually. If you end up in court."

"All you need to know is that I'm a teacher. I'm her teacher. And teachers take more than a superficial concern in their students' well-being."

"Well, the good ones do," he admitted. "But the problem with teachers is that they are often left alone with their students. So sometimes it's just your word against hers."

"So is that how it is? These days, a concern is interpreted as an inappropriate response?"

He leaned forward. "The social worker just couldn't find any evidence of what you're talking about. Miss Bolaris is not pregnant. There's no evidence that she ever has been. There's no evidence at all of abuse."

"Fine," I said. "Then I was wrong. But you can't blame me for wanting to know."

He nodded and stared at me, twisting back and forth in his chair.

"Can I go now?"

"Sure, you can go anytime."

I stood and he didn't. I waited. He was looking at me in a way that I'd seen before. As if I were some kind of pathetic specimen, a relic from the past, something he'd glimpsed before and might never see again.

"I suspect this will all blow over. But if I were you, I'd stay away from Miss Bolaris."

"That won't be a problem."

I walked through the bull pen, toward the place where I thought I'd first come in. The blood was ringing in my ears. When I got to the door, I was surprised to find Officer Mulligan had followed me. He opened the door for me.

He said, "You know, I'm a bit of a musician myself. Hacked around on the guitar when I was young. It was just never going to happen for me. My father is a cop, and his father was. This was always going to be my path. But I admire you people. I admire what you do."

"That's fascinating, Officer. You might have to find someone else to tell the story of your broken dreams."

"Oh, I don't think dreams really break, do they, Miss Swain? They just kind of move around."

I was standing in the parking lot, trying to remember where I had parked, when Hallie and her mother came out. Hallie saw me and averted her eyes. Dorothy followed her gaze and wasted no time in coming up to me.

"I hope you're happy," she said. "I trusted you."

I looked away from her. I stared at Hallie, who was concentrating on her shoes.

Dorothy said, "My husband is a well-respected man. The last thing we need is a scandal. So I'm more than willing to let this all go if you promise never to get within a hundred yards of my daughter again."

I trained my eyes on Dorothy at last.

"So now she's your daughter?"

"She told me everything. I know who you are. I know what I know."

"And I know what I know. Maybe we should just leave it at that."

"You artists. Real life is not enough for you. You just have to embellish, don't you?"

"I'm not an artist."

"Stay away from us. Do you understand?"

She marched away from me, and I watched her go. I stared at Hallie until I thought her skin might bleed. She wouldn't look at me at all. I walked away and I didn't turn, even after I heard her running toward me. She grabbed my arm and I still wouldn't turn.

She said, "Don't you see how you messed everything up?"

"Let go of me."

"They almost made me leave. I can't leave. I don't have anywhere else to go."

I still couldn't look at her. But I said, "I

tried to help you."

"I didn't ask you to help me."

"Sometimes people help without being asked."

"Yeah," she said. "But then it's not a gift. It's a burden."

I shook her hand off my arm and unlocked my car door.

I didn't look at her again until I had her framed in my rearview mirror. She was following Dorothy, her arms crossed and her head bowed to the ground. I saw, or thought I saw, a look of grim determination on her face. As if all of life was a battleground and she was planning her next move.

15

Nowhere in any biography I have ever read is there the chapter where the courageous but troubled protagonist decides to abandon her life's mission and focus instead on her affair with a twenty-eight-year-old bass player.

This is the course my life takes after my Christmas Eve encounter with Patrick. Any reservations I'd had about it in the past disappeared once he told me that I did not extend myself. It became my single-minded mission to prove him wrong.

So I extended myself with Clive. I extended myself in ways I had previously not thought possible. There are probably words in French to describe the ways in which I extended myself. It wasn't about love or even about sex. It was about "I'll show him." And it's possible that this course of action exists in every person's story, but the biographer wisely leaves it out. How admirable can it possibly be? How can it be explained in the course of someone's spiritual journey? But I am here to tell you that some of my best work, certainly my most creative work, was accomplished right there in my trailer park, after a round or two of margaritas or martinis. What I'm thinking is this: Certainly, great accomplishments have been sparked by a headstrong desire to prove someone wrong. Maybe all of them.

It isn't difficult to introduce Clive back into my existence. I simply swallow my pride and call him. I tell him I want to discuss the possibility of forming a band. He falls for the bait and comes over to my place. After a few drinks, he falls for bait of a different kind, and in the morning he sits up in bed, rubs his goatee thoughtfully, and says, "Hey, what about that band?"

"What about it?"

He grins and says, "There ain't no band, is there?"

"No, there apparently ain't."

He doesn't complain.

No one at work has a clue, least of all Franklin. He simply notes that I am in a better mood than usual and credits it, in fact, to Clive's absence.

"I told you that guy was bringing everybody down," he says.

I just smile.

He has hired a surly, washed-up forty-year-old session musician to take Clive's place. A woman, as it turns out. She is classically trained on the guitar but has abandoned it for the bass in recent years, and the fact that she is becoming uglier and surlier by the minute has driven her out of her chosen profession. No one was hiring her anymore, she complained to me as we stacked how-to videos together. They were jealous, she said, because she was too good at her craft. They were threatened. They hated women. They didn't understand the instrument. No one appreciated the bottom end anymore. She was just as devoted to the rhythm section as Clive, but her enthusiasm had decayed into a sour dismissal of all other instruments, and ultimately of music itself.

"It's all just bullshit," she says to me. Her name is Josie. She has a jaundiced complexion and doughnut-colored hair. She is shaped like a doughnut, too. This has earned her the name Krispy Kreme behind her back. (Ernest's creation. He likes to assign people nicknames behind their backs. Mine is Pearls Before Swine, just because it is easy and because I'm not supposed to know it. I never informed him that I'd endured a version of that nickname since kindergarten.)

"What's bullshit?" I ask her, just to pass the time.

"Music, that's what. We all act like it's a career. A valuable way to spend our time. But it's just an excuse not to grow up. There are people doing real jobs in the world. We're just fucking around. We might as well be doing finger painting for a living. It's schoolyard shit. Let's face it, we're all where we are because we didn't want to get a real job. Now it's too late to turn back. Hell, I can't even type. I'm stuck with music."

I like to hear her talk. She swears like a sailor, which is funny coming from a woman who looks like an embittered librarian. And I have endless patience for anything because I am getting laid on a regular basis by a man who has rock-hard abs and a seemingly permanent erection.

Patrick is giving me a wide berth at work. He seems to think he has gained some kind of upper hand with me. Occasionally I catch him smiling at me sympathetically, from across the room, as if he knows the mysterious origin of my deep sadness. What he doesn't notice, because he doesn't notice things, is that I have relinquished my deep sadness.

For about a month, I haven't talked to him at all. He is waiting for me to break. I don't break. One evening when we are closing up together, counting money in the cash register and sorting time cards, he says in a psychologist's voice, "How are you doing, Pearl?"

"I'm doing fine, Patrick."

He nods, as if he expects that kind of denial from me. Then he says, "Are you doing any work outside the shop?"

"A little," I say. It is true. I still do occasional session work and sit in with a country swing band once a month. But I know he isn't really asking about work. He is wondering if I am having a life. Extending myself.

"What about you?" I ask. "Are you moonlighting?"

He laughs, as if it is a ridiculous concept, and says, "One job is enough for me."

"Well, good. That's the best way to be."

When our work was done, we walk out together and he locks the door. He says, "Do you want to get something to eat?"

"No, I have to get home."

"What for?"

"I have a date," I say simply.

A look of surprise registers on his face before he can stop it.

"With who?" he blurts out.

"No one you know."

His face goes through a variety of expressions before he settles on indifference.

"That's good," he says in his psychologist voice. "I'm happy for you."

"Why?"

He laughs. "Why am I happy for you?"

"Yeah."

He shrugs. He doesn't know. This former physics professor who plays every instrument is stumped.

He says, "I don't think it's good for people to be alone too much."

"Good night," I say. And I walk away from him.

The funny thing is, he is right. And I am right. It's not nearly as much fun when both parties are right.

But that happens more often than not, I am forced to admit.

Clive can't let the issue of the band go. He mentions it when we are eating pizza in front of a Lakers game in my trailer.

He says, "I don't intend to spend the rest of my life teaching music. I want to do something, Pearl."

Clive is giving bass lessons from his apartment and in the homes of his students. It took him only a few weeks to match his salary at McCoy's, but he is now so busy he doesn't have time to pursue his own music. This is his constant complaint. I have endless patience for it. He is twenty-eight. He is supposed to long for something.

"I agree. You should do something," I say. "But you don't need me to start a band. What would a violin player do in a band?"

"Maybe you could learn to sing," he suggests. "Clubs pay more for bands with a chick singer. You're still hot. You could put on a miniskirt."

If you think I'm not flattered by being described as hot, you're wrong. Not to mention the idea that he is picturing me in a miniskirt.

"I don't sing," I tell him.

"I bet you could. Sheryl Crow isn't a great singer. She's just hot."

"She's young."

"You're not much older than her."

It occurs to me that he doesn't know how old I am.

I put my slice of pizza down and lean back into the couch.

"How old do you think I am?"

He shrugs. "That doesn't matter to me."

"Pick a number," I say.

He thinks. It's a struggle for him. Clive is

not a thinking man.

He says, "Thirty-four."

I laugh.

His smile fades. "What? Am I high or low?"

I am not an idiot. I won't give him a number.

His smile fades further. "How far off am I?"

"What difference does it make? Age is just a number," I say.

"You're right," he admits.

I kiss him, and the evening progresses, and sometime in the middle of the night, while we're lying too close together on my foldout couch, he says next to my ear, "Just give me a ballpark."

"Jesus, you aren't going to let this go."

"It won't make a difference," he says.

"Of course it will."

"I promise," he says, and his voice sounds quivery, like a teenager's.

Now I spend a few seconds thinking. Do I tell him? And what would be the problem in telling him? He might leave. I always knew he might leave, and I have made a halfhearted promise to myself that I won't care. What's more, I have a high-minded ideal that I want to be honest, want a man to accept me for who I am, warts and lines and accumulated wisdom and all. If I can't tell him how old I am, it diminishes our relationship in some important way.

It is in that moment that I realize I have grown attached to him. I never saw that coming.

I turn over to look at him. It's dark, but I can see the outline of his facial features. They are perfect in the way that all facial features are perfect before the judgment of time. His nose is a little crooked, but not too much, and his eyes sit where they should in the sockets — not sunken in yet, nor obscured by dark circles or puffy imbalances of fat. There are no lines, no creases. His goatee is as soft as a baby's hair. The rest of his beard is peeking through, but it is soft also, not stiff and grizzled the way a man's beard eventually gets. His eyebrows are smooth and obedient, not unruly and sprouting off in all directions. He is not old. He is not even mature. He is in the prime of his life, and looking at him in this moment I realize that I might be a little bit selfish, using up his best years in this way, when he believes I'm thirty-four.

The next thought that comes to me actually steals my breath. I think I might be a tiny bit in love with him. Not because he is young — youth has never really seduced me. I look at my young students with a degree of contempt, feeling that they aren't actually people yet because they have experienced nothing of any importance. Even Hallie, with all her hardships, struck me as someone who knew nothing about the roller coaster of life. I loved her in spite of her age, not because of it.

No, I am in love (if I am) with Clive because his laughter sounds like a fountain trickling, and because he delights in small victories (such as when the pizza arrives on time and hot), and because he cares to a ridiculous degree about the rhythm section (he goes into a fugue state when I put on a Jimi Hendrix or Little Feat record), and because he tells funny stories and laughs at my jokes, and because he knows how to fix his own car, and because he watches the news with a serious expression on his face, as if it is all true and it all matters, and because he remembers that I like to be kissed on the back of my neck, and because he puts the toilet seat down, and because he's very quiet in the morning when he leaves, so he won't wake me. Clive is a lovable person, not just a good lover, and I have secretly fallen under the spell of him, and now I am in a horrible place, the place I never like to find myself, wherein I have something to lose.

The moment that I realize I am invested in him, and in his opinion of me, I also realize that I am not playing games. I have lost my original intention, to show Patrick or Franklin or Mark something, and now I am engaged in a relationship, if you interpret the concept, and I do, as a situation in which two people are dependent upon each other for certain needs.

"Forty," I say.

His face stalls. Everything about him stalls. He says, "Forty what?"

I laugh. "Forty years. I'm forty years old."

"Get out!" he says.

"You can leave now," I tell him. He might as well. It's a trial, the two of us attempting sleep in these close quarters, in this thing that doesn't even qualify as a bed. I am going to miss him.

He raises himself up on an elbow. He looks like Adonis, I promise you, in the pale light that is spilling in through my one window. His chest is smooth and broad and muscled. He smells good, like some kind of soap, and I can't resist the urge to run my fingers through his soft hair, one last time.

He says, "Why would I leave?"

"Because. I'm forty."

He leans forward and kisses me hard on

the mouth, in a way that actually scares me some. It's a determined kiss, almost an angry kiss, and I wonder if he's going to hit me. I wonder if he's going to say something like, You bitch, you led me on.

Instead, he pulls me on top of him. He is strong. I am caught off guard. I say, "What are you doing?"

"What do you mean?" he asks. "We're awake, aren't we?"

"But I'm forty."

"That just makes it better," he says.

I bury my face against the soft skin on his neck.

16

I have a new student. His name is Lance. He is eleven years old and can play the violin like someone who was born to do it. He is shorter than he should be, and his hair is platinum blond and he has pale blue eyes and dimples. He is not angry or frustrated, and his parents are extremely middle-class. His mother is a nurse; his father is a car mechanic. They can afford his lessons, though just barely, and the only thing his mother ever says to me when she drops him off for lessons is, "Tell us how we can help him develop his talent. We want this for him."

It is almost too good to be true, and it takes the place of the hole that Hallie left in my life. Lance does not have the fire that she did. Nor does he have the heartbreaking backstory. But he is good, he likes to work, and he listens to everything I tell him. I can see how it will unfold. I will keep on teaching him until his late teens. Then he and his parents will decide he needs to pursue this further, and they will take him away from me. There is nothing much to hook into. He is simply going to be my charge for a few years, and then he will move on.

I don't mind this for the same reason that I don't mind anything. Because I am with Clive. Because just about every evening, I can go home and fall into the arms of a young man who thinks it is fabulous that I'm forty. Our relationship is progressing. He wants me to meet his parents. Fortunately, they live in Arizona now and don't come out much. But Clive is preparing for the day. He wants to get us out in the open. He wants to make us official.

I like that, but some days I am confused by it. I can't really have a future with him, yet I am thoroughly unwilling to give him up. He is getting me through this life. He is making the ugliness of my existence go away. Surely we are going to hit a roadblock. Surely, any day now, the exact number of my age will register with him and he will realize how impossible it is.

For example, Clive wants to have children, and he brings it up now and then. I say, "I'm too old for that."

He tells me how he's read articles in *Newsweek* that assure him a woman can have a baby into her fifties if she's motivated. I don't tell him that it takes a certain willingness on the part of the woman. Sometimes he tries to talk me into abandoning birth control (we're still using condoms because we're both too lazy to get tested). When he does that, I say, "Clive, I have no desire to be pregnant."

He says, "My friends with babies tell me life doesn't even start till you have them."

I say, "My friends with babies tell me that life ends when you have them."

"Oh, you're just being weird," he says.

The discrepancy is moving in on me. He wants; I don't want. He expects; I have given up on expectations. I accept, and he just desires, late into the night, scanning the ceiling with his young and hopeful eyes.

When I start teaching Lance, I start staying at the store later and later. I have started teaching him two nights a week, more often than I usually teach students. He has soccer practice three times a week, so I have to make allowances. On Mondays and Wednesdays, I stay until seven o'clock, teaching him. That means I don't get home until eight. Sometimes I find Clive pacing in front of my trailer, smoking, irritated, anxious.

He doesn't reprimand me, and I always joke him out of his bad mood or lift his spirits by bringing home pizza or Chinese food. He is so young he can actually be won over by such things. Young people have short attention spans, and I have learned how to use this in my favor. We don't fight much because I can deflect his anger or frustration without much effort, and in the rare instances when he clings to something, I can always coax him away from it with sex.

It's so easy, I think sometimes, daydreaming as I drive to work. It's almost too easy. There can't be any future in it because I have too much of the upper hand.

I am looking for reasons to destroy this. Because it feels too much like happiness. I'm no stranger to it, of course. I was happy with Mark. I don't want to go there again.

What's the higher calling — art or music?

This is the discussion I wander into right before Lance comes in for his Wednesday session. Josie has taken the side of art, just to annoy the others, I assume, and I opt to side with her for the same reason. But for a long time, I just listen.

"How can you say that?" Franklin asks, taking the bait. "Art is just slopping paint

270

on a canvas. Music is really creative. It serves an actual purpose."

"Purpose my ass," Josie says. "It's all bullshit."

"Did it ever occur to you," Franklin says, his eyes turning beady with rage, "that music is the only thing that makes any sense and the rest of the world is bullshit?"

"I used to think that, too," she says. "But I'm the one who's actually had some success as a musician, and I'm telling you, it's ultimately bullshit."

"Oh, I haven't had any success?" Franklin spits back at her. "I'm in a band."

Ernest rescues him from that flimsy defense by saying, "What would the world be without Stevie Ray Vaughan or Lynyrd Skynyrd? Sure, life would go on, but would you want it to?"

"I wouldn't give a flying fuck," Josie says.

"Well, you're just pissed off," Ernest counters, as if it were a medical condition.

"I think what Josie means is that music is a kind of luxury," I say. "An accoutrement. It doesn't solve problems or advance evolution or contribute to world peace."

"Oh, and art has helped us evolve?" Franklin asks.

"Well, you know, the cave paintings are

pretty important. They helped record history."

"Music stopped the Vietnam War," Franklin says.

I have to laugh. "Okay, come on. Some good music came out of that era, but it didn't stop anything. The Defense Department stopped that war because it wasn't politically or financially expedient."

"Whose side are you on?" Franklin asks.

"I'm not on anybody's side. I just see her point. She's saying we elevate music to a level that it cannot support. That's why we're all so miserable. We can't put it in perspective."

Josie nods at me, as if I'm the only person on earth who understands. She doesn't realize I'm only supporting her to keep the argument alive, because I am a person who enjoys fireworks.

"Art," Patrick suddenly says from across the room.

We all turn to look at him. He's leaning casually against the wall, his arms crossed, smiling at us with that anemic expression of his, from that superior middle ground.

"That's just bullshit," Ernest says in his twang. "You can't even talk about this because you aren't even a musician."

Patrick ignores that and looks deliberately

at me. "Explain it, Pearl," he says.

"Me?"

"You know how it goes. Sound waves vibrate at a lower frequency than colors. Art requires light. And what's the speed of sound compared to the speed of light?"

"I don't know the exact numbers, though I'm sure you do."

"They aren't in the same ballpark. Sound is retarded compared to light."

"But who says faster is better?" I ask.

"I don't think we're talking about faster. We're talking about higher. What's the higher calling? Colors vibrate on a higher frequency."

Franklin looks dumbfounded. He says, "You two are just babbling now."

"Music is math," Patrick says. "Art is vision. You tell me which is a higher calling. Music requires instruction. Art cannot be taught."

"Sure it can," Franklin says. "You've never heard of art school?"

"No great artist ever went to art school," Patrick says. "Every great musician went to music school."

"Hendrix didn't," Franklin says. "He couldn't read a note of music."

"Well, that opens up the debate as to whether or not he was great."

"It's all bullshit," Josie says, wanting back into the argument, though she is lost.

"What about playing by ear?" I ask Patrick. "What about the people who don't need the math?"

"I don't believe those people exist," he says. "I think they are lying."

"But you claim to be one of those people," I counter.

"I never did."

See, here it comes. He denies that our night together ever happened. I am stranded with my perception of reality.

"You said that you play every instrument."

He remains calm, though I've blurted out his secret. He says, "No. I said I *can* play any instrument. If I choose. Because I know the math."

Franklin has had enough. He goes to the wall of guitars and grabs one. He thrusts it at Patrick and says, "Play."

Patrick just grins. Franklin thrusts the guitar again, as if it is a gun. And Patrick, for some reason, backs up. As if he, too, is convinced that it is a lethal weapon.

"Play, goddamn it. Let's have this out, once and for all."

Patrick laughs. "Is this a duel?"

"Yeah, it sure as hell is. Play."

The chimes on the door jangle, and then

Lance and his mother are standing in the room, looking at this curious configuration of people and events.

"Are we early?" Lance's mother asks.

"No," I say. "Right on time."

She nods to Lance, who goes up the stairs. Franklin puts the guitar back on the wall. Patrick sighs and walks over to the cash register as though to hide behind it. Josie and Ernest scatter to different ends of the room.

"I feel like I interrupted something," Lance's mother says.

"Nothing important," I say.

Lance is crying when I come into the lesson room.

He looks up at me, his pale face blotchy, tears streaking his cheeks.

"What in the world?" I say.

He sniffs and holds the violin toward me. A string is broken.

"Oh, Lance," I say, fighting the urge to laugh. "You broke a string. It's no big deal."

"I was trying to tune it," he explains.

"Well, you shouldn't do that. I haven't taught you how yet. It's very tricky."

"They're expensive," he tells me.

"Yes, they are," I admit. And I know he is scared because he realizes his parents can't afford it. I think of Hallie and her unholy exchange for the cost of music lessons. I won't let that happen to anyone else. And I am momentarily filled with rage that music costs money. It should be free, available to everyone.

"I've got some strings in my case," I tell him. "I'll give you one. But you should be more careful."

He sucks in a breath and says, "My parents don't know. They'd get really mad."

"They'd get mad at you for breaking a string?"

He shakes his head.

"Then what?" I ask.

"The voices," he says quietly.

"What voices?"

He suddenly sits up, looking strong and eager. It's my willingness to hear him that is giving him strength. He says, "I hear the voices. They tell me what to play. They told me to tune the D string. I do what they tell me. That's how I learn."

My throat feels dry and I sit back in my chair, trying to disguise my alarm. I want to hear this, but it suddenly feels as if everything that happens in my lesson room ends in a bizarre kind of disaster. Every student I touch goes a little bit crazy.

"What kind of voices?" I ask.

"They sound like people voices. I used to think it was just me talking to myself. But now they have started telling me to do things I don't want to do. I didn't want to tune the string. But I listened, and it went bad. I don't think they are on my side anymore. I used to think they were angels, but angels wouldn't make me break a string, would they?"

I am thoroughly unqualified for this, just as I was unqualified to handle Hallie's problems. I made the mistake of overstepping the bounds with her. I am not going to do it with Lance.

And yet, I do. I say, "Sometimes I hear voices, too. Not voices so much, but a kind of instruction, telling me what notes to hit. I call it intuition. I think that always happens in music. You don't have to be afraid of it."

"It makes me nervous," he admits. "I like to tell my parents about the stuff that happens to me, but I can't tell them this."

"Tell me. I'll listen."

He wipes his face with his sleeve. He is starting to calm down.

I'm still a little worried about the voices, so I say, "They don't tell you to do anything else, do they?" I'm thinking of Son of Sam.

He shakes his head. "They only start when

I pick up the violin."

"I just think that is inner guidance. It's not bad or evil. It's not even strange. Just learn to make friends with the voices."

"But why would the voices tell me to do something wrong?" he asks, his own voice still laced with childish pain.

"Maybe they didn't. Maybe they told you the D string needed tuning. Maybe you took the next step and tried to do it yourself."

He nods slowly, as if this makes a certain kind of sense.

Even as I'm talking, I realize I sound a little crazy. The thing is, I believe him, and I believe myself. I know. I have known for a long time that music has its own secret language. I know that if you don't hear the secret language of guidance, you probably aren't a musician.

What I'm not sure of is whether it is appropriate to say this to an eleven-year-old boy. But I can see the sadness lifting from his face, like fog lifting from the ground, and after a few moments we are sailing through the scales and everything is back to normal.

17

I am sitting in my car on a dark street in Mar Vista, looking at the power lines weaving through the limbs of some unidentifiable tree, wondering why the tree limbs don't catch fire, wondering why I don't know the answer to that, marveling at how nature and technology have adapted to each other, relatively speaking, and trying to imagine what the world must have been like before Isaac Newton.

It is hard to imagine, for example, that for a very long time, people did not understand about gravity. It is even harder to imagine that people still don't understand about gravity and that gravity is just a theory, a pretty good one until something else comes along. The way bleeding people was state-of-the-art medicine till antibiotics came along. It makes me wonder this: If someone disproved the theory of gravity, would we all go floating off into space? Do we cling to the earth because we believe we should? Impossible, you say, because people stuck to the earth before Isaac Newton, but that was because they believed something else, such as that the earth was flat. My point is, how much of how we live is predicated on and dependent upon our collective consent, a mutual belief system, a vision we're all having, a tune we are all hearing in somewhat the same way?

When Isaac Newton first started talking about optics, people were so shaken, I've heard, that they began committing suicide en masse. I've heard that about other great discoveries, too. It sounds completely irrational, but I'm afraid to admit I understand it a little. When I read about string theory and time travel and cloning and nuclear fusion and the phasing out of the post office and gene therapy and on and on, it makes me glad I am not going to live forever. I feel relieved. I'd rather not know. This must be how those people felt in Newton's time. Everything was changing too fast. The printing press was enough of a shock. Then the planets moving around the sun, then the Cartesian split, then gravity, then all of color actually being derived from white light. I'd rather not know, they must have said.

Think how it must have felt to be Newton. Every new idea in his head — and the ideas must have been coming at him like a swarm of bees — changing the basic structure of science and the very foundation of the collective belief system. Every time he opened his mouth, someone either praised him to heaven or jumped off a building. No wonder he finally stopped talking about his discoveries. He burned his most extensive writings on optics. The smartest thinking anyone has ever done on the subject, ashes at the bottom of his fireplace. It wasn't that it scared him. It was that he must have known, on some level, that no one else could follow it. So what was the point?

Newton burned his knowledge because he didn't want to be a freak. He wanted to belong. We all want to belong. But when we are cursed with knowledge, we start looking for an exit.

I don't know what I'm doing here, parked on this street, thinking of Isaac Newton, until the front door of the familiar house opens and Hallie comes out. Then I know. I have to see her. I wasn't sure I would, but here she is, just as I remember her, only a little older. Her hair is longer, but other than that, she is exactly the same. She doesn't look like the girl I accosted on the street in Venice, so that really was a departure from reality. Okay, I say to myself, I own that. I was just trying.

It could have been her. She could have changed herself and changed back. I don't know anymore.

It is too dark to see if she is wearing an eyebrow stud, or if she is smiling, or if she is miserable. She is wearing jeans and a sweatshirt and is lugging a Hefty bag full of garbage. She is staring at the ground as she walks toward the big brown garbage bin parked at the curb. I watch her as she struggles with the lid of the garbage bin, then shoves the Hefty bag into it. She wipes her hands on her jeans, then looks straight up at the sky. I look, too. There is nothing up there but a pale half-moon and some asthmatic stars struggling to be recognized. I wonder what she thinks of them. I wonder if she is dreaming about something. I wonder if she has anything left to wish for.

Then she looks in my direction, though it is impossible to tell if she's seeing me. I freeze, as if I have just been caught at something degrading, even illegal. Whatever the illegal thing was that she almost accused me of. Was she right and I wrong? It was a long time ago, but did I really just hunt her down to prove or disprove my own sanity?

My heart begins to race as she walks in my direction. Fool, I think, fumbling for the keys in the ignition. But I can't start the car because that would draw further attention to me, and anyway, I don't want to go. I want to wait right here as she moves closer and closer.

She stops a few feet from my window. She is definitely looking at me now, but without a hint of recognition in her eyes. The eyebrow stud is still there. But her face is a blank. I don't know what I am going to say to her. I realize, to my horror, that all this time that I've been agonizing about her, I could easily have found her. It wasn't even a matter of looking. I knew where she lived. I knew her phone number. I could have followed up. I could have written her a note. I could have done a lot of things. But like those people who jumped off the roof in Newton's time, I would rather not know.

She taps on the passenger-side window with her knuckle. I roll the window down and we look at each other, there under the shadow of the unidentifiable tree and the distant hum of the power line.

"Hey," she says.

"Hey," I say. We are forcedly casual and awkward, like teenagers, which only one of us can legitimately claim to be.

"What are you doing here?" she asks.

"Looking for you," I answer honestly.

"What for?"

"I just wanted to know . . ."

I hesitate, unsure of how to finish the sentence, until I realize that it is finished.

She smirks. She understands. I want to know, and that might be my curse. If it is, then it is a curse I share with much of humanity. Imagine that. I'm just like other people. At least, I am like those people who choose not to jump off a building, who choose instead to wait around and see what will happen.

Isaac Newton was from a poor family. His mother abandoned him. He was basically a welfare kid. He was a second-class citizen at Cambridge, earning his keep by waiting on other students. He listened to his teachers. He allowed himself to be taught. But the ideas he came up with, which would change the world forever, simply came to him, as if whispered in his dreams.

"Are you all right?" I ask her.

She shrugs, then spreads out her arms, as if to exhibit her wholeness, the fact that her limbs are still attached to her body and everything is in working order.

"You see me?" she asks. "You see that I'm okay?"

I don't take that bait.

"What about Earl? Is he still around?" I ask. I don't know how else to put it.

"He still lives here, if that's what you mean."

"But is he . . . are you . . ."

"He leaves me alone," she says.

"But he didn't always?"

"It wasn't like you imagined."

"Hallie, I don't think I imagined anything."

"You never did understand," she says.

"I tried. I think you wanted me to try."

She shrugs.

"How could you have said those things about me?"

She shrugs again. "There are flaws in the system."

"You could have gotten me in real trouble. And it wasn't true."

"It wasn't entirely untrue. I mean, you did care about me more than you needed to. It freaked me out."

"How can you put a value on caring? I cared."

"Well, I just wasn't used to that."

We are silent for a moment. Finally I look up at her.

"How about your music?"

"I don't play music," she says. "I don't

need it anymore."

I have no response to that. She shoves her hands in the pockets of her jeans. She is hiding her hands from me. She doesn't want me to look at her wrists. It is a hold I have over her, this knowledge of her talent. It is something that cannot be forgotten. But to remind her of it is an abuse of power. This is what she is saying to me.

She says, "Look, I've got another year here. I can stand it. Then I'll get a job. Or I'll go to Europe. Something like that."

"Hallie," I say quietly.

"Look," she says again, her voice shifting up this time. She is angry or frustrated or scared. It all looks the same in the dark, and I have never been able to read voices the way I can read notes. People confuse me. Their sounds are complex and conflicting. They always seem out of tune. I hear people's sounds, but I can't interpret them.

She says, "You just have to get over me, Pearl. Leave it alone."

It's funny how she says it. As if I am the abandoned one and she is asking me to move on. I feel humiliated and rejected. But encouraged, too, in a strange way. Hallie is telling me to move on. Hallie is saying my work is done here. This is probably what I came for.

So I tell her, "I want to know you're okay. I handled it badly. I'm sorry. It's my fault. I should have been more understanding. I shouldn't have pushed."

These words are coming out of me in a torrent. They sound rushed and confused and younger than my years, younger than Hallie's years.

She smiles, and her smile seems calm and comforting. It reassures me. I have come here to be reassured by my student. How sad is that? I feel my tongue backing down my throat and tears are shoving at the corners of my eyes.

She says, "It's okay. You just wanted me to be great. But I don't want to be great. My mother was that way and it drove her nuts. She died."

"You're looking at it all wrong," I say.

"I have to go inside," she says.

"Hallie, just don't give up."

"Why would I do that?" she asks.

"Please. Talk to me."

She shakes the hair out of her face, and suddenly she appears mature. Way more mature than I am. She has a knowing look in her eyes.

She says, "Things mostly work out. People have their stories, you know? All the calamity and drama, it's a way of putting things off. It's an excuse not to live."

I don't say anything to that.

She says, "Look, how it happens is, people survive stuff. Everybody's story is sad because people like sad stories. But the truth is, we just work our way through the mess. I probably told you stuff I shouldn't have. I was probably trying to get you to care. And you proved you cared."

She starts backing away. I want to leap out of the car and grab her. I want to kidnap her and take her home. I want to shape her life. I want her to amount to something. I think it is my job. I watch her retreating into the shadows, and I realize there is nothing I can do.

I think, She is going to be okay. Then I think, No, she is not.

Then I realize she is going to be okay some days, and some days she is not, and that is how it goes.

Out the window, I say, "Hey, was that you I saw on the street in Venice?"

She laughs. "Face it, you're just going to keep seeing me."

"Until what?" I ask.

"Until you don't need to anymore."

I get out of my car but stay next to it. "Did you get anything from me?" I ask. I hear the scared, pathetic tone in my voice. Like when you hit the wrong note on a violin. It's sorry for you. It wants to make it up to you. It translates your pain.

Hallie turns. She says, "Too soon to tell. But it's over now, you know? Everything ends. You move on to the next thing."

"Tell me what to do."

She's in the shadows now. I can barely see her. But as always, I can hear her.

She says, "Don't be pathetic. I couldn't live with that."

I stand there for a long time after she's gone. I hear the whir of the power lines.

Finally I get in the car and close the door.

I start the engine and I hear the pistons churning, and I turn the headlights on and see the rays illuminating the road ahead of me, and I'm in the presence of all these laws of physics, which have always governed our lives, even when we didn't understand them, and I know that awareness improves and diminishes our lives in equal parts.

I put the car into gear and I move away from her and toward something else.

18

When I get home, I am greeted by the angry, pacing version of Clive. We have not made a plan to get together tonight. We said we would call each other. So I am surprised, agitated, pleased, and annoyed to see him, all at once.

"It's cold out here," he says as I get out of the car. It is late February, and the rainy season has set in. It hasn't actually rained today, but the clouds have been hovering and the threat of rain feels just like the actual event in L.A.

"Yes, it's a little chilly. What are you doing here?" I ask.

"It's Wednesday. We usually see each other on Wednesdays."

"I had Lance today. You know I stay late when I have Lance."

"So it's all about Lance now," he accuses. I actually laugh; it's such a ridiculous charge.

"No, it's only about Lance on Wednesdays."

"And sometimes on Mondays."

"What's your point, Clive?"

He obviously doesn't have a point. He stuffs his hands in the pockets of his jeans. One reason he is cold is that he is not wearing a coat. People can't get a handle on the weather in Los Angeles, even if they were born and raised here. It claims to be a warm climate, but it is not. And its attitude changes as drastically as hormones.

He thrashes around for a point, then comes up with this: "You have to decide if we are a couple or not."

"All right. I'm going with yes, we are a couple."

This surprises him. He hesitates a moment, then says, "Well, couples make time to see each other."

"I have some time now," I say, kissing him on the neck. I had targeted his mouth, but he turned his head away at the last second.

"You are wearing me out," he says.

"How am I doing that?"

"You act like you want to be with me, but you won't really be with me."

"How can I be more with you, Clive?"

"You could meet my parents, for one thing."

"Give me a time and a place."

"That's just an example."

I am starting to feel angry now. I am starting to think he's not worth it. I am tired from my lesson with Lance and my encounter with Hallie, and I really just want to have a beer, eat some peanuts, and crawl into bed with the TV remote. I would like to have sex, but I am resenting all the layers I have to work through to get there.

I remember, now, why love is so difficult. You have to process another person's feelings. I find it challenging enough to process my own. You have to see into the future a little bit to love someone. You have to anticipate their concerns, feel their feelings, and formulate an appropriate, and often forced, response.

At the same time, I know that if I reject this thing in front of me, I will end up like Josie or Ernest or Franklin or Patrick. I will become smug and self-righteous. I will have all the answers without even considering the questions. I will observe life and construct elaborate theories. I will put forth these theories and ridicule anyone who refuses to validate them. I will start to stoop or gain weight, and I will start to rant. I do not want this for me.

I take Clive by the hand. It is stone cold,

but it starts to warm up as my fingers wrap around his. I say, "Come inside. You're just cold and hungry."

"Don't try to confuse me," he says.

"I won't. Just come inside."

He follows me without arguing. Once we are in the trailer, he collapses in a chair and I open a can of chili. I'm not really hungry, but I know once the smell permeates the small trailer, Clive will start to calm down.

As I'm fixing him a tray, he says to me, "Pearl, I can't decide if you are my future, or if you're interfering with it."

This might be the smartest thing I've ever heard from him. It's so smart that I can't formulate a response. So I put the tray down in front of him — a steaming bowl of chili, with some shredded cheese and corn chips on the side, along with a bottle of beer. He looks at it longingly, but he seems to understand that if he takes it, he will have lost another battle.

"Well, let's look at the options," I say. "I could be both. I could be neither. Or I could just be the person who is going to keep you from being alone tonight. All of those things are pretty good."

He takes a few bites of chili, then puts his spoon down and looks at me again.

"I'm afraid I'm in love with you, Pearl," he says.

"That's okay."

"Do you ever feel that way?"

"Yes," I admit without hesitation.

"Doesn't it scare you?" he asks in an exasperated tone, as if this were the worst imaginable predicament.

"Of course it does."

"Then why don't you look scared?"

I smile. "I am older than you. Fear doesn't bother me as much."

He stares at me for a long moment, then goes back to eating the chili. He eats slowly, but without pausing, without looking up, without speaking. Finally he puts his spoon down in his empty bowl, wipes his mouth with the paper napkin, and looks up at me.

He says, "Why don't you introduce me to any of your friends?"

I laugh. I light a cigarette and wave the smoke away so it won't annoy him. Which is foolish, because there is nowhere else for the smoke to go in this confined space. He doesn't seem to notice.

"You know all my friends," I tell him. "Franklin, Ernest, Patrick, Declan."

"You don't have any other friends?"

"Well, there's Ralph, the drunk next door. I could invite him over sometime."

"You don't have any girlfriends?"

The realization dawns on me that I have not thought about Leah in sometime. I saw her long enough to get permission to sleep with Clive. And to invade Pearl's life. I have divorced her. He's right, I have kept this part of my life away from him. And from myself.

"I have one girlfriend," I say. "Her name is Leah. You can meet her anytime you want."

He nods, and his body seems to relax, as if he is slowly but surely getting to the bottom of this particular mystery.

"What about your parents?" he asks. "Why don't you want me to meet them?"

"Because they're dead," I say.

His eyes widen and he leans forward in his chair.

"Oh, my God," he says. "I'm sorry."

I shrug and smoke my cigarette.

"Both of them? When did they die?"

"Years ago," I say.

"When you were a kid?"

"No, when I was an adult. I'm forty, Clive. A lot of people my age have dead parents."

He stares hard at me, as if this is something he is unwilling to accept. I'm not sure whether he's trying to fathom the reality of my age or the reality that everyone dies. Or maybe it's a simultaneous awareness dawning on him, and being with me is going to remind him, every moment of his life, of the relentless passage of time. The advantage to being with someone your own age is that you confront the specter of mortality at the same pace.

"So you're an orphan," he says.

And my immediate response is to laugh, though my laughter soon dies and I stare back at him, letting my cigarette smolder away as I contemplate his words.

It's true, I am an orphan. Hallie was an orphan. Was this part of our connection? Is this, in fact, the lingering connection? If so, it has taken me a long time to see it.

"Everyone is eventually an orphan," I say. "Unless they don't outlive their parents. But everyone expects to do that."

Clive hears this, and he thinks about it, but I can't help him. He is young and he is hearing a terrible truth. That life is about painful realization. It's about parties for a long time, and then someone has to pick up the tab. He sees the tab but he can't reach for it yet. Seeing the future is so much more difficult than not seeing it. That's what Isaac Newton would say. Maybe it's even what Hallie would say. Maybe it's what I would say if I weren't glimpsing something more real.

"I'm sorry about that," Clive tells me. "I'm sorry for you."

"Don't," I say. "Don't do that to me."

"Don't what? Feel badly for you?"

"Bad," I snap. "You feel bad, not badly. If you feel badly, it means you have no nerve endings in your fingers."

He just stares at me. I realize two things: that I have veered off into parts unknown, and that I have rejected an honest emotion. It makes me feel bad. Bad, not badly.

I stub out my cigarette and kneel down in front of him. I take his hands into mine. He avoids looking at me. I have shamed him. I don't know why I do that to people.

"I'm sorry," I say. "But you can't go around making people into victims. You can't pity people. Especially if you love them."

He lifts his eyes to mine. "Why?"

"Because the goal is to elevate the people you love. You know, make them better. Make them strong. Expect things from them."

While he is thinking about this, I feel my mind racing back, again, to Hallie. I expected things from her. And I drove her away. I turned her into something monstrous. I devalued her with my expectations. I negated her. I did that.

But I couldn't have done that. I wanted everything for her. I wanted to help.

The thing I didn't see back then is that people can be destroyed by goodness. Damage can be done by hope. If people aren't ready for hope, it's a cruel trick to put it on their doorstep. Like a bag of shit on fire. They stomp it out because they don't know what else to do.

I don't know how to say this to Clive, and I am glad. Glad that I can't say it, glad that he wouldn't understand it. Glad that our relationship is so off balance that I cannot disrupt it any further. All I can do is be in it.

He sighs and rubs his eyes, the way a kid does when he is past the point of exhaustion. He blows the breath out of his lips, and they drum together as if he's trying to make bubbles or create a new sound.

He says, "I don't know, Pearl. I feel kind of lost sometimes."

"Yeah," I say.

"Like, I can close my eyes and see my whole future coming together. I can see me in a band or writing songs and recording them in a studio. At the same time, I see me being this totally conventional guy, with a wife and kids and dogs and stuff. They're both me, but in a way, neither one of them is me. It's just a guy I'm imagining."

He stops talking and stares. I know better than to speak.

Then he says, "Sometimes I can't see my future at all. Like it's a complete blank. I try to picture it, but nothing comes."

I nod. He waits. There is nothing to say.

"Do you ever think about the future?" he finally asks.

"Not much," I answer honestly.

"Why?"

"Because I don't believe in the future."

"Oh, right," he says, with a slight eye roll. "There is only now. Don't get Zen on me."

"But there *is* only now. It's not a Zen thing. It's something I believe. It's more like physics."

"Tell me," he says.

"Well, some scientists believe that everything is happening at the same time. The past, the present, and the future. It's all the same thing. It's one big cosmic soup. It's a kind of perpetual motion. Do you understand?"

He shakes his head, but I keep talking.

"It's the idea that there is no linear time at all. It's all just a perpetual state of now. Like billions of TV screens with the same program on, but at different times. Past and present both affecting each other, but the moment itself never changes. It just is. And there is nothing else."

"There's nothing else," he says slowly, "because we could get hit by a truck tomorrow."

"Well, yes, but we could also never have been born. According to this theory."

"So, like, nothing is real?"

"Nothing is real, and nothing is not real. Things just are. That's why you try to be in the moment. Because you might as well be somewhere. And all evidence seems to point to the fact that being here, now, is where all the good stuff happens."

He nods and stares at my hands, which are still holding his.

He says, "Like when you're playing a riff, and you're not worried about finishing it. You're just in it."

"Right."

He takes one of my hands to his lips and kisses it. Something like an electric current shoots through me. There is a feeling in it, and the feeling makes me want to forgive everyone and forget everything. I am reminded that I am alive, and that might be enough of a thing to be.

He says, "Also, this could all be a dream."

I smile. "Well, like Bob Dylan said."

His face draws a blank. He doesn't know much about Bob Dylan. That's okay, too.

"What did he say?" he asks.

"I'll let you be in my dream if I can be in yours."

Later when we are in bed, huddled together against the cold (as if it were possible to do anything in that bed except huddle), I let my eyes roam across the ceiling and I think of Lance and his voices. The whole exchange seems like something I imagined and willed into existence. He is the first student who has ever talked to me about the voices. Hallie hinted at a similar kind of intuition, but I drew my own conclusions about her. I knew she could hear the music in her head. I knew she didn't have to read it. But that was another thing altogether.

It is true that I have heard similar voices in my life. As Lance said, it isn't exactly a human voice, and it isn't even what we think of as language. It is more like energy, or some kind of intelligence, offering suggestions. Then I translate that intelligence into language that I can understand. The best way to describe it is that it is like a song, but that is misleading, too, because we think of songs as things that already exist, created by people. But where do songs come from in the first place? A tune is not a thing you can construct; it is a thing you deconstruct by putting it into notation, or by rendering it on an instrument. It loses something in the translation. It starts out divine, and as soon as a person touches it, interprets it, it becomes something else. It is not so much despoiled as transfigured into something both human and divine. Like Jesus. Perfectly human and perfectly divine.

I am starting to understand the meaning of this, as I lie very still next to my twenty-eight-year-old lover, whose soft breathing sounds like a primitive kind of music. Music is everywhere. He breathes in a constant, steady rhythm, as it makes sense for a bass player to do. And maybe that is where rhythm comes from, I think. Our earliest understanding of rhythm. The sound of our own breath, the beating of our own hearts.

ACKNOWLEDGMENTS

Thanks to the people who helped me find the music: Dave Marsh, Howard Yearwood, Jonathan Grossman, Laurie Gunning Grossman, Jeffrey Allen, Adam Levine, and all the Enablers. Thanks to the people who wouldn't let me stop: my editor, Chuck Adams, and my agent, Cynthia Manson. Finally, thanks to the people who put up with me for free: Karen, Faith, Lyla and Sharon, Craig and Jen, Kevin, and Troy.

ABOUT THE AUTHOR

Barbara Hall is the award-winning creator of two successful television series, *Judging Amy* and *Joan of Arcadia,* as well as a frequent contributor of scripts for such outstanding series as *I'll Fly Away, Moonlighting,* and *Northern Exposure.* In addition, she is the author of eight previous novels, five of them for young adults. She lives in Los Angeles.

The employees of Thorndike Press hope you have enjoyed this Large Print book. All our Thorndike, Wheeler, and Kennebec Large Print titles are designed for easy reading, and all our books are made to last. Other Thorndike Press Large Print books are available at your library, through selected bookstores, or directly from us.

For information about titles, please call:
(800) 223-1244

or visit our Web site at:
http://gale.cengage.com/thorndike

To share your comments, please write:
Publisher
Thorndike Press
295 Kennedy Memorial Drive
Waterville, ME 04901